TWISTED JOURNEYS® #8

ALIEN INCIDENT ON PLANET J

DAN JOLLEY

ILLUSTRATED BY MATT WENDT

GRAPHIC UNIVERSE™ · MINNEAPOLIS · NEW YORK

Story by Dan Jolley

Pencils and inks by Matt Wendt

Coloring by Hi-Fi Design

Lettering by Marshall Dillon

Graphic Universe
A division of Lerner Publishing Group, Inc.
241 First Avenue North
Minneapolis, MN 55401 U.S.A.

Website address: www.lernerbooks.com

Library of Congress Cataloging-in-Publication Data

Jolley, Dan.
    Alien incident on Planet J / by Dan Jolley ; illustrated by Matt Wendt.
       p.   cm.—(Twisted journeys)
    ISBN 978-0-8225-6998-5 (lib. bdg. : alk. paper) 1. Graphic novels. 2. Plot-your-own stories.
[1. Extraterrestrial beings—Fiction. 2. Science fiction. 3. Plot-your-own stories. 4. Graphic novels.]
I. Wendt, Matt, ill. II. Title.
    PZ7.7.J65AI 2008

    [Fic]—dc22   2007044116

Manufactured in the United States of America
1 2 3 4 5 6 – DP – 13 12 11 10 09 08

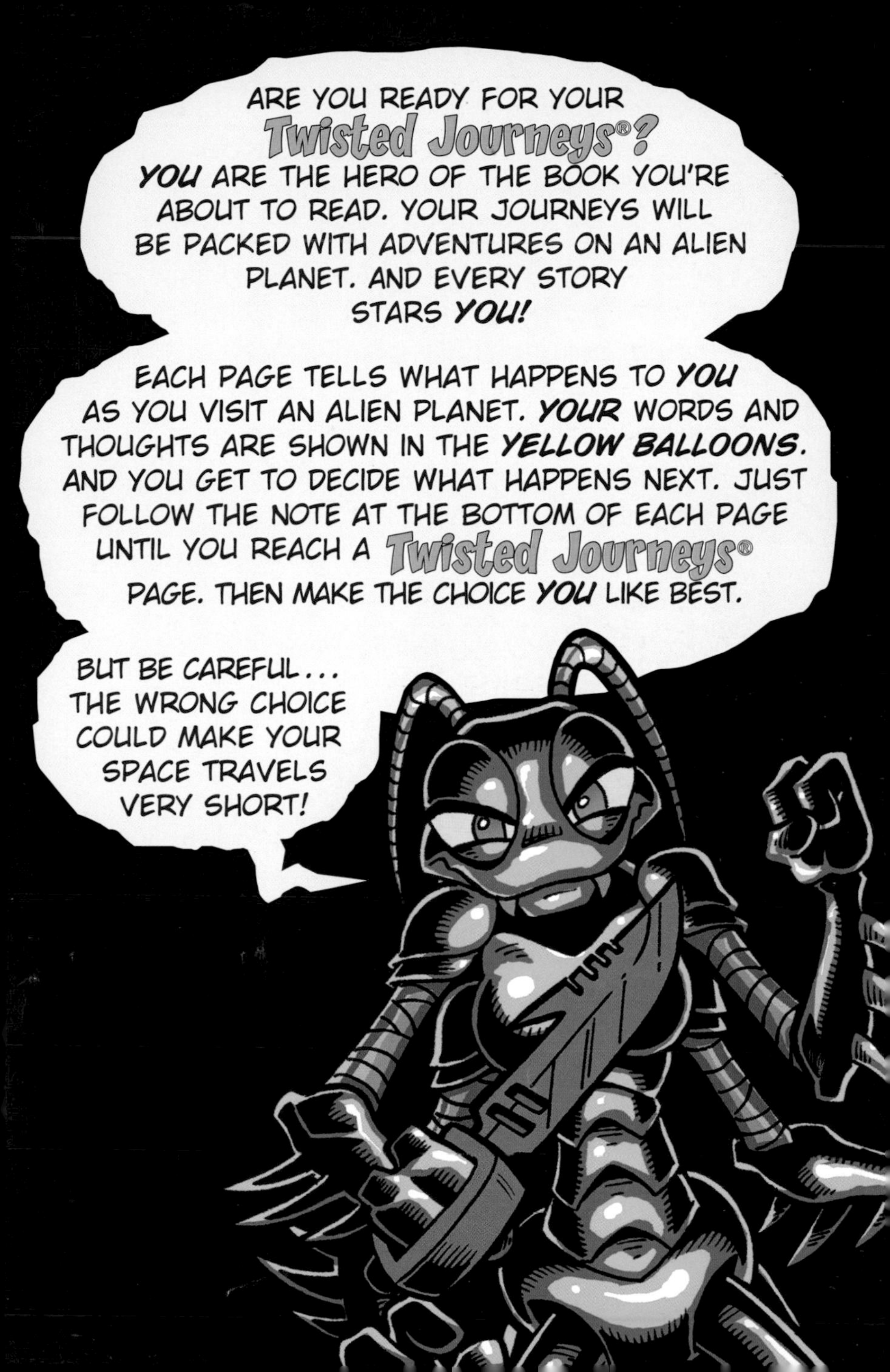
ARE YOU READY FOR YOUR Twisted Journeys®? YOU ARE THE HERO OF THE BOOK YOU'RE ABOUT TO READ. YOUR JOURNEYS WILL BE PACKED WITH ADVENTURES ON AN ALIEN PLANET. AND EVERY STORY STARS YOU!
EACH PAGE TELLS WHAT HAPPENS TO YOU AS YOU VISIT AN ALIEN PLANET. YOUR WORDS AND THOUGHTS ARE SHOWN IN THE YELLOW BALLOONS. AND YOU GET TO DECIDE WHAT HAPPENS NEXT. JUST FOLLOW THE NOTE AT THE BOTTOM OF EACH PAGE UNTIL YOU REACH A Twisted Journeys® PAGE. THEN MAKE THE CHOICE YOU LIKE BEST.
BUT BE CAREFUL... THE WRONG CHOICE COULD MAKE YOUR SPACE TRAVELS VERY SHORT!

"We're landing *where*?"

"You heard me," your mother says. She puts the spacecraft into automatic landing mode. "Jarfarkarlarquillar."

You look out the viewport at the barren hunk of rock you're zooming toward. "I don't think I can pronounce that," you tell her. "I think I'll just call it Planet J."

"Call it whatever you like," she says. "But we have to set down there and get a new wormhole analyzer, or this dinky little spaceship your father insisted on buying won't be going very far."

You adjust your lucky hat and watch as Planet J gets closer. "Okay. So what's this place like?"

"Well . . . let's just say you're going to need the holo-projector your granddad built. It's been about ten years since anybody here has even seen a human. We'll be a lot better off if we keep a low profile."

Cool! You haven't had a chance to use one of those before. This was supposed to be just a routine trip to visit Granddad, but this stop along the way might turn out to be kind of fun!

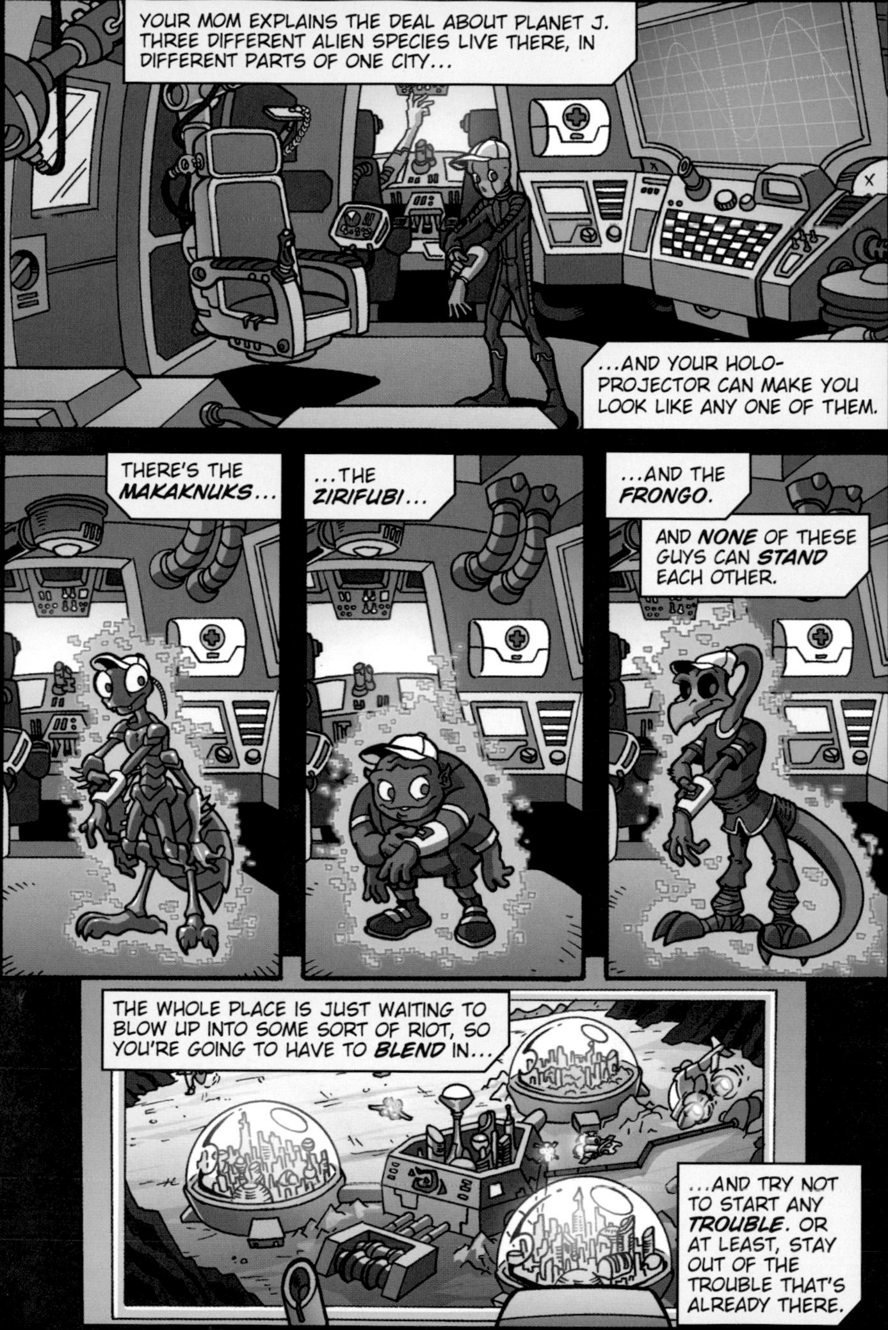
YOUR MOM EXPLAINS THE DEAL ABOUT PLANET J. THREE DIFFERENT ALIEN SPECIES LIVE THERE, IN DIFFERENT PARTS OF ONE CITY...
...AND YOUR HOLO-PROJECTOR CAN MAKE YOU LOOK LIKE ANY ONE OF THEM.
THERE'S THE MAKAKNUKS...
...THE ZIRIFUBI...
...AND THE FRONGO.
AND NONE OF THESE GUYS CAN STAND EACH OTHER.
THE WHOLE PLACE IS JUST WAITING TO BLOW UP INTO SOME SORT OF RIOT, SO YOU'RE GOING TO HAVE TO BLEND IN...
...AND TRY NOT TO START ANY TROUBLE. OR AT LEAST, STAY OUT OF THE TROUBLE THAT'S ALREADY THERE.

GO ON TO THE NEXT PAGE.

The ship settles down and docks with no problem.

"I have to stay here on the ship and talk to the spaceport officials," your mom tells you. She puts some money in your hand, along with a spare set of keys to the ship. "I'm trusting you to get the wormhole analyzer. Go to the first shop you see, but don't get one that's overpriced. I want some change back!"

The spaceport looks pretty much like others you've seen.

To your right, there's a huge, six-sided metal door that makes you think of a honeycomb.

Over to your left, there's another big door, but it looks as if it's made of wood, with leafy green vines draped over it.

As the doors open and close for travelers, you can tell the six-sided door leads to the Makaknuk part of the city, and the wooden one goes to the Zirifubi section. Judging from the way these places look, and by the people coming and going, you think you could get a used part for cheap in the Makaknuk section . . . or a brand-new but more expensive part in the Zirifubi section.

GO ON TO THE NEXT PAGE.

WILL YOU . . .

. . . try to save a little money?
TURN TO PAGE 30.

. . . go with the idea of getting what you pay for?
TURN TO PAGE 8.

You head for the doors to the Zirifubi section, adjusting your holo-projector as you go . . .

. . . and *wow!* This part of the city is *beautiful*. It's sort of like walking into a rainforest with streets and buildings and cars. You see Zirifubi everywhere, going about their business. It all looks pretty peaceful. You head down the street, looking for a used-parts shop.

GO ON TO THE NEXT PAGE.

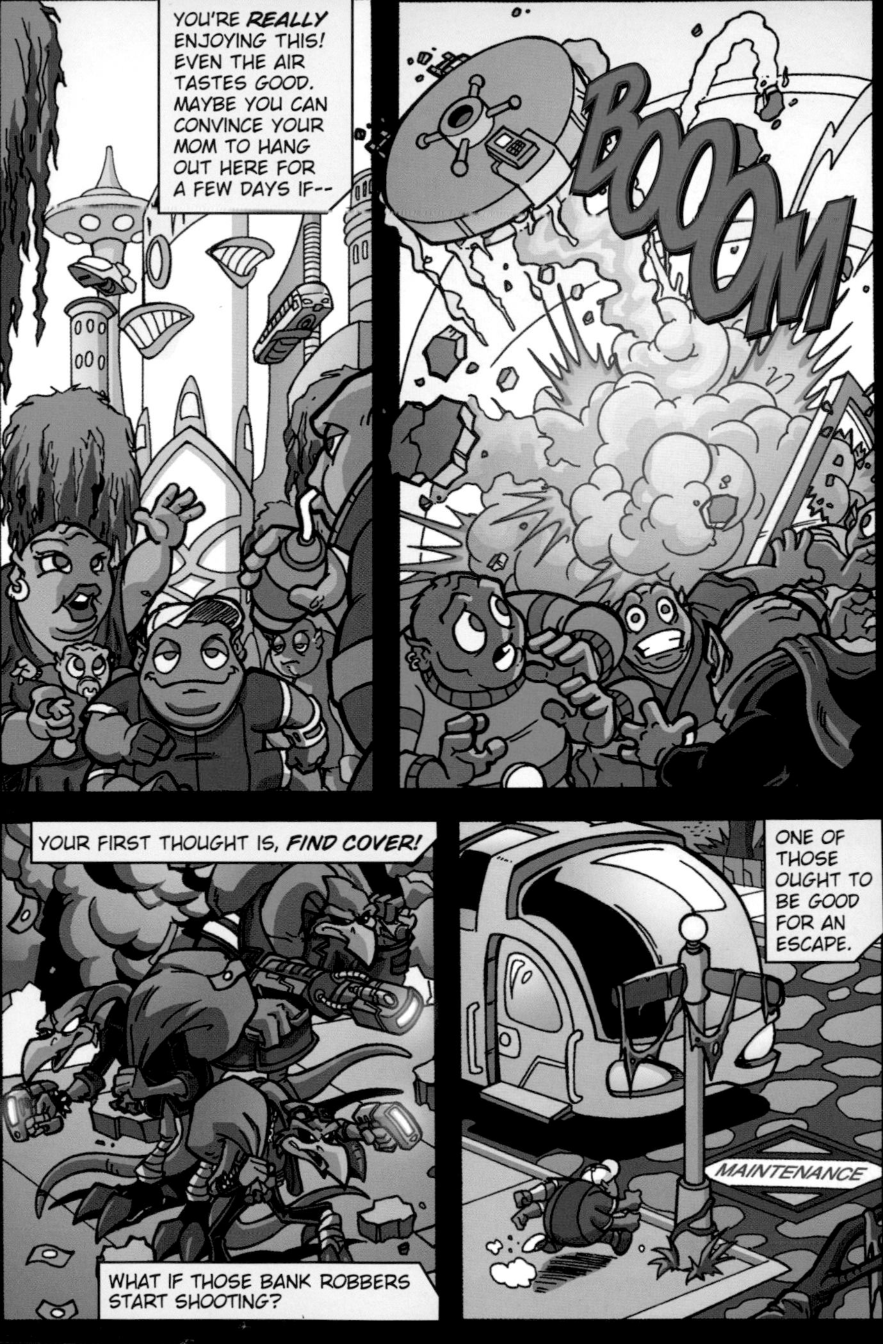
YOU'RE REALLY ENJOYING THIS! EVEN THE AIR TASTES GOOD. MAYBE YOU CAN CONVINCE YOUR MOM TO HANG OUT HERE FOR A FEW DAYS IF--
BOOOOM
YOUR FIRST THOUGHT IS, FIND COVER!
WHAT IF THOSE BANK ROBBERS START SHOOTING?
ONE OF THOSE OUGHT TO BE GOOD FOR AN ESCAPE.
MAINTENANCE

GO ON TO THE NEXT PAGE.

You've got to hide!

WILL YOU . . .

. . . climb down into the maintenance tunnel?
TURN TO PAGE 58.

. . . hide under the bus?
TURN TO PAGE 16.

What's the one thing these guys won't expect? Makaknuks, that's what! You switch your disguise to one of the big alien bug creatures. The leader shouts in surprise. "What is this?"

"This is your only warning!" you shout, doing your best to sound convincing. "The Makaknuks won't take any more of this foolishness! All Frongo-on-Makaknuk crime will stop this instant. And don't think we won't be *watching you*."

You head for the exit. You're hoping if you act like you know what you're doing, they'll let you just walk out.

But no such luck. You're only halfway there when the leader stops believing your act. "The child is lying!" he screams. "Shoot! *Everybody shoot!*"

Every Frongo in the place draws a gun. You're surrounded. But hey, it was a good bluff. It *almost* worked!

THE END

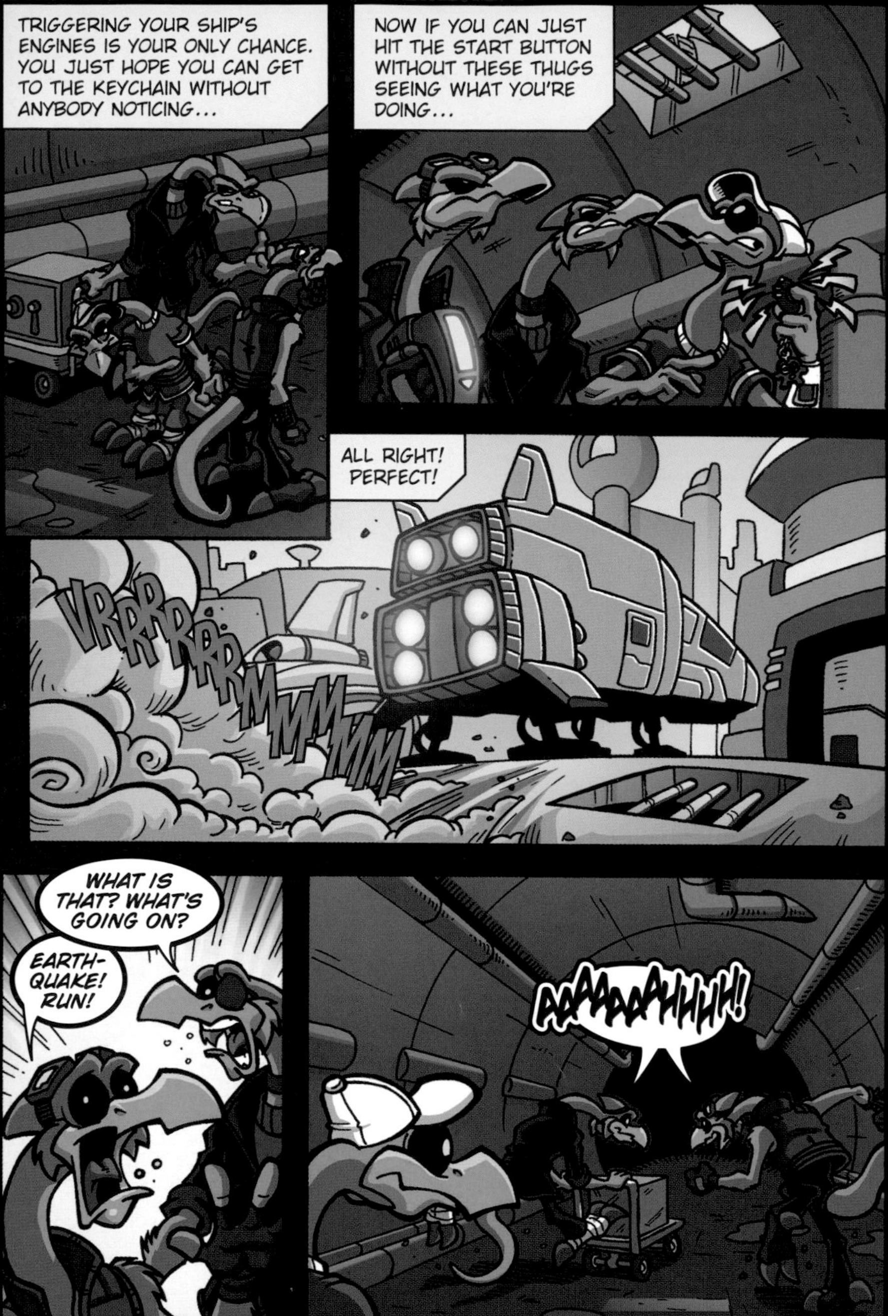
TRIGGERING YOUR SHIP'S ENGINES IS YOUR ONLY CHANCE. YOU JUST HOPE YOU CAN GET TO THE KEYCHAIN WITHOUT ANYBODY NOTICING...
NOW IF YOU CAN JUST HIT THE START BUTTON WITHOUT THESE THUGS SEEING WHAT YOU'RE DOING...
ALL RIGHT! PERFECT!
VRRRRRRRMMMMMM
WHAT IS THAT? WHAT'S GOING ON?
EARTH-QUAKE! RUN!
AAAAAAAHHHH!

GO ON TO THE NEXT PAGE.

The two Frongo thugs are gone for now, but you don't know if they're coming back. Better get out of here while you can.

You spot a maintenance ladder running up the side of the tunnel, right up to the edge of the metal grate. You click the key chain again and shut off the spaceship's engines, and then you scamper up the ladder.

Mom already knows you're in trouble when you get inside. You guess your engine trick tipped her off. She bundles you into the ship and straps you in without even deactivating the holo-projector. Before you know it, she's engaged the engines and the two of you are lifting off.

"But, Mom," you say, "what about the wormhole analyzer? Don't we need that?"

"Yeah," she tells you. "But not bad enough to stay on that planet a second longer! We'll find one some- where else!"

That's good enough for you!

THE END

There's no telling where you're going to end up if you just sit here. As discreetly as possible, you try to pull your legs up so you can jump clear of the sidecar—

—but the driver sees you moving! "Hey!" he shouts. "Hold still! Don't you move!"

You'd better do something *right now*, before he hits you with that stun thing again . . .

. . . so just as you cross a bridge over a canal, you fling yourself out of the sidecar.

A second later you hit icy cold water with a huge splash.

GO ON TO THE NEXT PAGE.

The canal isn't that wide, but it looks deep, and the walls are high.

WILL YOU . . .

. . . swim along with the current and hope you can find a place with lower walls?
TURN TO PAGE 56.

. . . head to the left, where the water looks murky but the wall is closer?
TURN TO PAGE 34.

. . . try to make it to the right wall, where a huge building hangs over the canal?
TURN TO PAGE 23.

You dive under the bus and get out of the way of any debris that might still be flying around. You can see people's feet as they run past, but you're feeling pretty safe here . . .

. . . until the engine starts up and the bus begins to rise *straight up* into the air. It's a hover-bus! You don't have time to think about finding anyplace else to hide, either, because one of the legs of your holo-projector suit has gotten caught on a snag of metal. The bus keeps rising—and suddenly you're rising with it!

"Help! *Help!* Get me down from here!" you scream, but there's no answer. The bus takes off down the street, way above the ground, with you dangling from the underside.

You'd enjoy the view of the city if you weren't hanging upside down and in fear for your life.

GO ON TO THE NEXT PAGE.

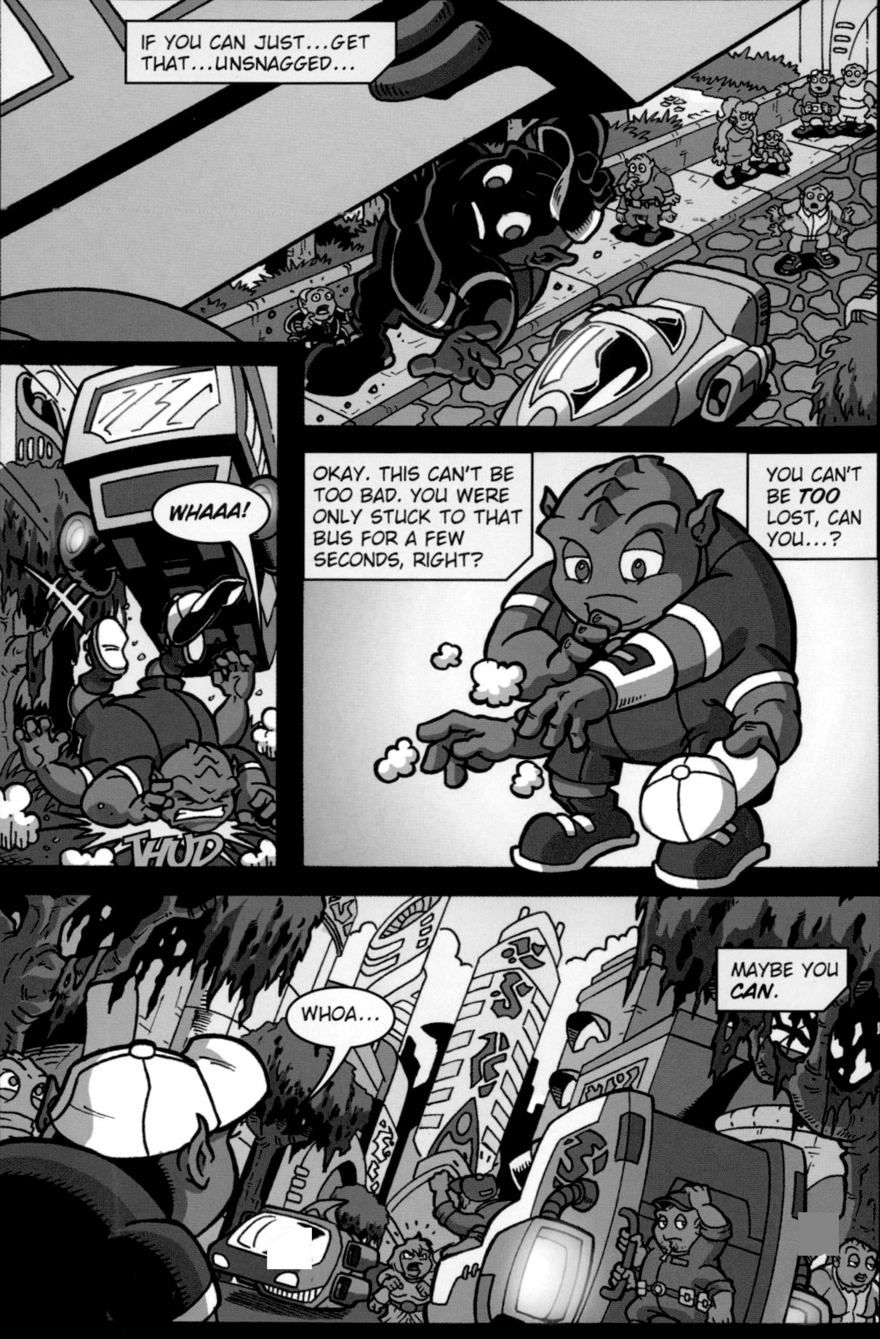

IF YOU CAN JUST...GET THAT...UNSNAGGED...
WHAAA!
THUD
OKAY. THIS CAN'T BE TOO BAD. YOU WERE ONLY STUCK TO THAT BUS FOR A FEW SECONDS, RIGHT?
YOU CAN'T BE *TOO* LOST, CAN YOU...?
WHOA...
MAYBE YOU *CAN*.

GO ON TO THE NEXT PAGE.

So now you're alone and lost
and surrounded by aliens.

WILL YOU . . .

. . . start walking back the way
you think you came?

TURN TO PAGE 20.

. . . try to phone your mom at the spaceport?

TURN TO PAGE 44.

. . . ask a pedestrian for help?

TURN TO PAGE 103.

You feel a little bit dazed. Going back to the fire alarm, you hit the button again, and the red lights shut off. Then you use the phone to call your mom. "Stay right there!" she says. "I'm coming to you! Don't move!"

You hang up the phone and wander out into the room where the three criminals were plotting together. For the first time, you notice a big pile in the corner, covered over with a tarp. You've got some time to kill . . . so you go over and peek underneath.

It's a huge pile of brand-new, shiny wormhole analyzers.

You sit down and start laughing. They're probably stolen . . . but, you figure, when you tell the police how you accidentally got rid of the city's terrorist leaders, maybe they'll let you keep one.

From outside you hear sirens approaching.

Man, your granddad is never going to believe *any* of this . . . !

THE END

At first you really enjoyed the Zirifubi section of this city, but now it just looks weird and scary. You get the feeling everyone is staring at you. Can they see through your disguise? You look down at your hands. Nope, they look like big toad hands to you. So you keep going and try to act like you belong there.

Pretty soon the street you're on forks: One way turns to the left, the other to the right. You don't remember this intersection . . . but then, you *were* upside down and going pretty fast.

On the left, the street has a row of restaurants, with names like Shalizi's All-You-Can-Eat Larva Bar and Gushbrush's House of Fungus. On the right you see four or five small movie theaters, advertising titles like *600 Brides for 600 Brothers* and *My Webbed Foot*.

GO ON TO THE NEXT PAGE.

Left looks just as good as right,
as far as you can tell.

WILL YOU . . .

. . . turn left and head down Restaurant Row?
TURN TO PAGE 107.

. . . turn right and see if maybe you can get some
movie popcorn to eat while you're walking?
TURN TO PAGE 37.

It's desperate, but it's worth a shot: You switch your disguise to a toadlike Zirifubi. There's a gasp from the crowd, and the Frongo leader growls deep in his throat.

"Sorry for the misunderstanding!" you tell him. "I'm, ah, see, I'm a documentary filmmaker. A student, actually. I'm making a documentary student film about the lives of the Frongo, and, y'know, I just thought I'd try to blend in . . ."

The leader thinks. Then, slowly, he asks you, "If you're a filmmaker . . . then *where* . . . is your *camera*?"

Argh! You hadn't thought that far ahead! "I . . . uh . . . I . . . was on a preliminary fact-finding mission?"

The leader doesn't believe you for a second. He orders you held captive while he demands a ransom for your return. The thing is, you know your mom doesn't have the kind of money they're asking for!

It's going to be a *long* wait.

THE END

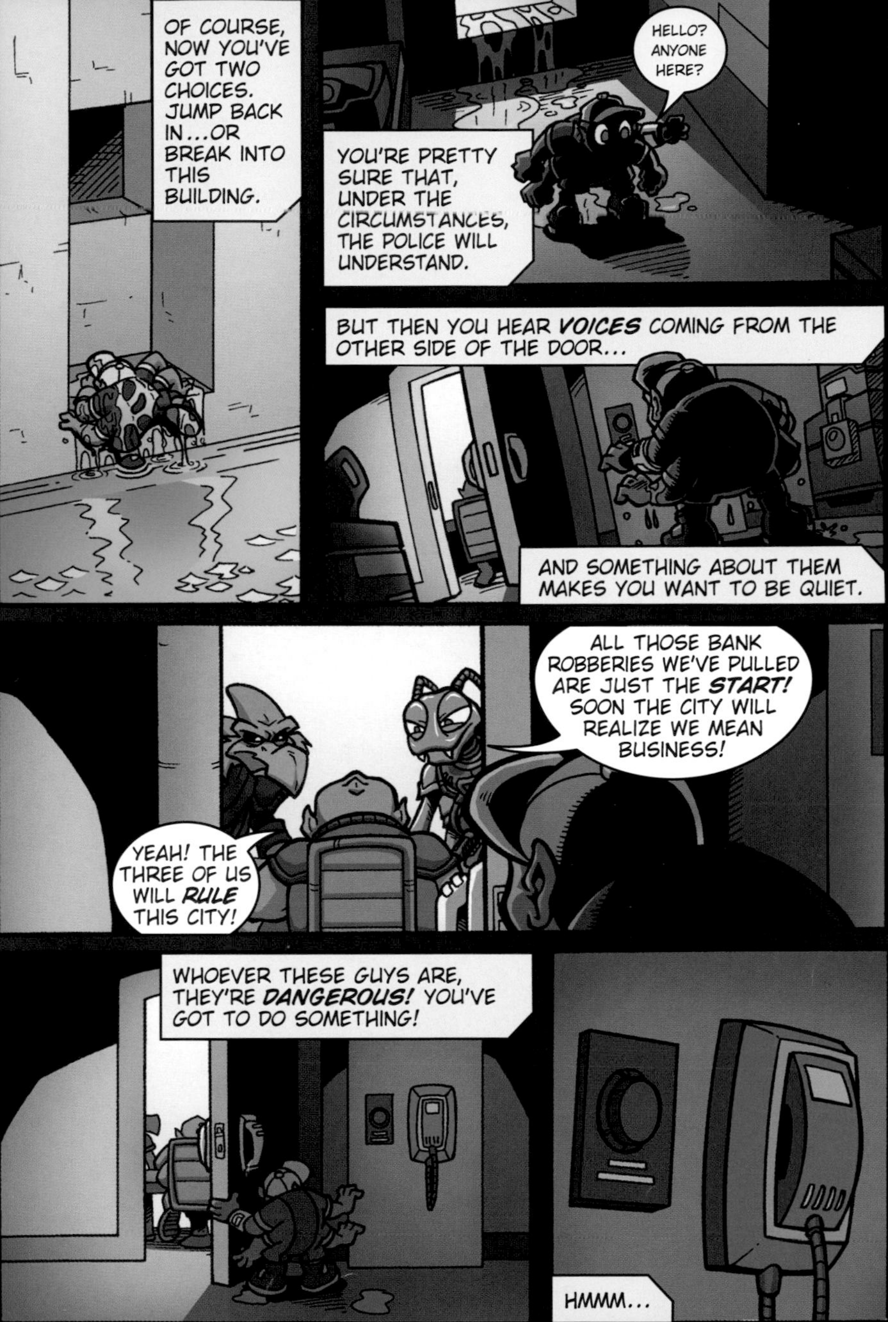
OF COURSE, NOW YOU'VE GOT TWO CHOICES. JUMP BACK IN...OR BREAK INTO THIS BUILDING.
HELLO? ANYONE HERE?
YOU'RE PRETTY SURE THAT, UNDER THE CIRCUMSTANCES, THE POLICE WILL UNDERSTAND.
BUT THEN YOU HEAR VOICES COMING FROM THE OTHER SIDE OF THE DOOR...
AND SOMETHING ABOUT THEM MAKES YOU WANT TO BE QUIET.
ALL THOSE BANK ROBBERIES WE'VE PULLED ARE JUST THE START! SOON THE CITY WILL REALIZE WE MEAN BUSINESS!
YEAH! THE THREE OF US WILL RULE THIS CITY!
WHOEVER THESE GUYS ARE, THEY'RE DANGEROUS! YOU'VE GOT TO DO SOMETHING!
HMMM...

GO ON TO THE NEXT PAGE.

Those three might be the root
of all the problems here on Planet J.
You know you've got to do *something*.

WILL YOU . . .

. . . use the phone to
call your mom?
TURN TO PAGE 84.

. . . sneak into the room and
stop them yourself?
TURN TO PAGE 92.

. . . hit that big red button
and see what happens?
TURN TO PAGE 100.

No way are you going to stand there and let them grab you. You take off running, aiming to put as much distance between you and them as possible . . .

. . . but the crowd keeps getting in your way. Everywhere you turn, there are more weird toad creatures, either running away themselves or trying to stop the ones who *are* running. You can't take more than two steps without having to stop and change directions.

That's when you hear the amplified voice behind you. "Hey! You in the white hat! Stop right there!" You glance over your shoulder and see a Zirifubi soldier coming up out of a roof hatch on the vehicle. He has a megaphone in one hand and a rifle in the other. "Do not move until we collect you!"

Then someone bumps into you, and too late you realize they've jostled the holo-projector switch over to "FRONGO."

"Spy!" someone screams, pointing at you. The cry goes up all around you: "Spy! Spy!"

And the soldiers close in on you, weapons ready to fire . . .

THE END

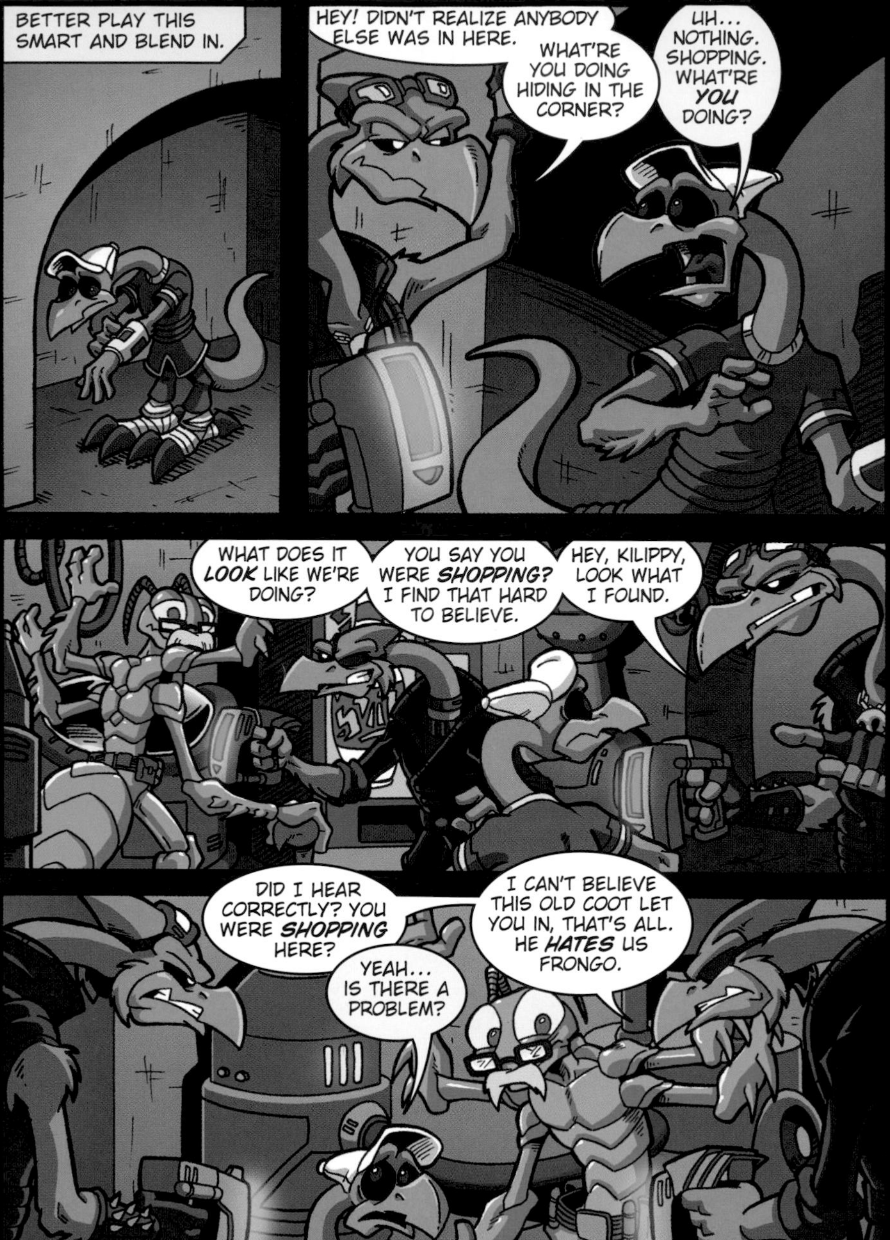
BETTER PLAY THIS SMART AND BLEND IN.
HEY! DIDN'T REALIZE ANYBODY ELSE WAS IN HERE.
WHAT'RE YOU DOING HIDING IN THE CORNER?
UH... NOTHING. SHOPPING. WHAT'RE YOU DOING?
WHAT DOES IT LOOK LIKE WE'RE DOING?
YOU SAY YOU WERE SHOPPING? I FIND THAT HARD TO BELIEVE.
HEY, KILIPPY, LOOK WHAT I FOUND.
DID I HEAR CORRECTLY? YOU WERE SHOPPING HERE?
YEAH... IS THERE A PROBLEM?
I CAN'T BELIEVE THIS OLD COOT LET YOU IN, THAT'S ALL. HE HATES US FRONGO.

GO ON TO THE NEXT PAGE.

Kilippy gets a gleam in his eye. "Well, since we've got company, why not make the best of it? You can help us rip this place off."

You splutter for a second. "Wh-what? You want me to help you rob the shop?"

"That's what I just said, isn't it?" Kilippy seems impatient. "Here, take Old Man Honest into the back room and keep an eye on him. If he tries anything funny, give a shout—" he raises his gun "—and we'll come back and barbecue him." Kilippy pokes Honest Broknuk, urging him toward the back room. "Bet you'd taste like lobster, huh?"

Honest Broknuk doesn't put up any fuss as you take him into a small back room. "Third time this month," he mutters. He seems pretty discouraged.

GO ON TO THE NEXT PAGE.

"Listen, sir, I'm going to help you get out of this," you whisper to Honest Broknuk.

"Oh, don't put yourself out on my account," he says. "I don't think they're going to hurt me. The Frongo have been bothering the Makaknuks for years, and it seldom gets serious."

"Well, seldom is still too often," you tell him. "We'll figure something out."

"Hey!" Kilippy's voice rings out from the front of the store. "Mystery shopper! Get out here and give us a hand with this safe!"

"Go on," Honest Broknuk says. "I'll be fine. Just be careful, all right?"

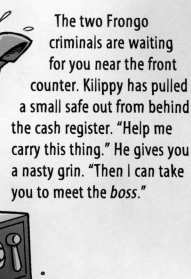

The two Frongo criminals are waiting for you near the front counter. Kilippy has pulled a small safe out from behind the cash register. "Help me carry this thing." He gives you a nasty grin. "Then I can take you to meet the *boss*."

For now these thugs don't seem to want to hurt you, but that could change any second.

WILL YOU . . .

. . . make a break for it and sprint out to the street?
TURN TO PAGE 46.

. . . cooperate and go with them?
TURN TO PAGE 52.

You figure a used part is just as good as a new one. You're just going over to Granddad's place, right? You set your holo-projector to Makaknuk and head toward the six-sided door.

The huge door splits open to let you through, and it's like walking from one planet onto another. It's still a city—there are buildings and roads and people walking around. But everything has a sort of greenish shine to it . . . and while it all looks sort of cheap, everything is so *neat* and *clean* and *well organized*. It's kind of like walking into some weird alien museum.

You see a sign hanging outside a shop nearby:

GO ON TO THE NEXT PAGE.

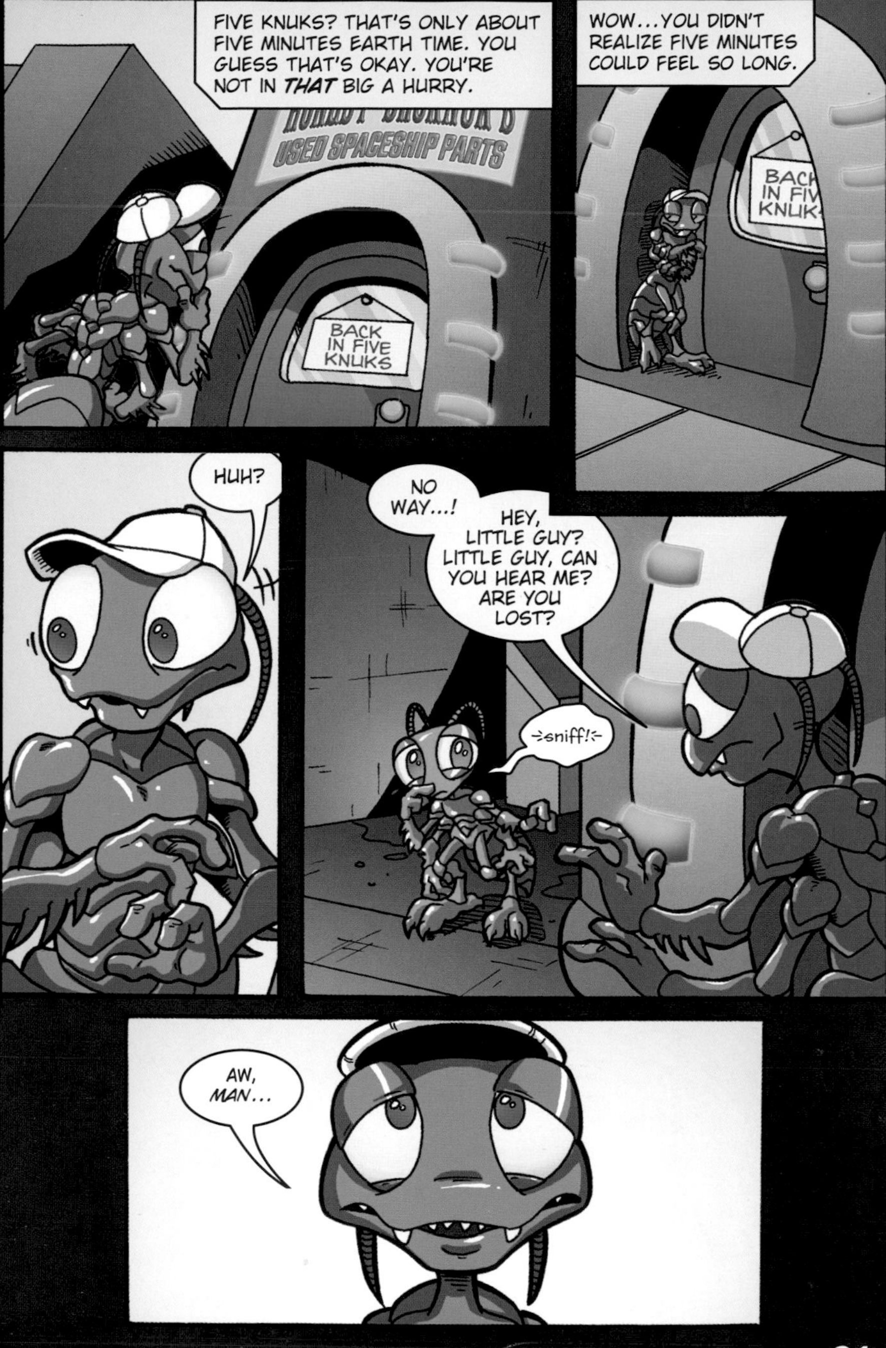
FIVE KNUKS? THAT'S ONLY ABOUT FIVE MINUTES EARTH TIME. YOU GUESS THAT'S OKAY. YOU'RE NOT IN *THAT* BIG A HURRY.
USED SPACESHIP PARTS
BACK IN FIVE KNUKS
WOW...YOU DIDN'T REALIZE FIVE MINUTES COULD FEEL SO LONG.
HUH?
NO WAY...!
HEY, LITTLE GUY? LITTLE GUY, CAN YOU HEAR ME? ARE YOU LOST?
sniff!
AW, MAN...

GO ON TO THE NEXT PAGE.

You're on an alien planet, in an even more alien part of the city. You *know* you don't know what's going on. But that little kid might really be in trouble!

WILL YOU . . .

. . . go try to talk to the kid and find out if it's okay?

TURN TO PAGE 40.

. . . stay here, but keep an eye on the kid to make sure it stays safe?

TURN TO PAGE 48.

"Dr. Sprigmarsh," you say slowly, trying to figure out the best way to do this. "I'm not sure what you've heard about Earth kids, but I'm—*OH MY GOSH LOOK OVER THERE WHAT IS THAT THING?!*"

Sprigmarsh whirls around with a yelp. "What? What? What is it? What thing where?"

But you haven't even waited for him to finish babbling confused questions. There's a door in the far wall, and you beat feet toward it with all haste.

Sprigmarsh recovers faster than you expected him to, though. "Stop where you are!" he yells. "Don't move a muscle!"

"Not a chance, creepo!" you shout back. "I'm outta here!"

"No, you don't understand!" He waves his arms frantically. "The security system is still armed! If you touch that door—"

But it's too late. Your hand's already on the doorknob . . . and as 75,000 volts course through you, it's very clear that this is

THE END

You think the left canal wall might be closer, so you start swimming for it with all your strength. It's tough going. The canal's current is pretty swift, plus the water itself is *incredibly* cold. But little by little, you get closer to the wall, and you start looking for a ladder or something to climb out with.

That's when you feel the current shift around you . . . and you see something dark in the water below.

Something *huge*.

You *really* don't want to think too much about what sort of creature might live at the bottom of a canal on an alien planet. You start swimming harder.

GO ON TO THE NEXT PAGE.

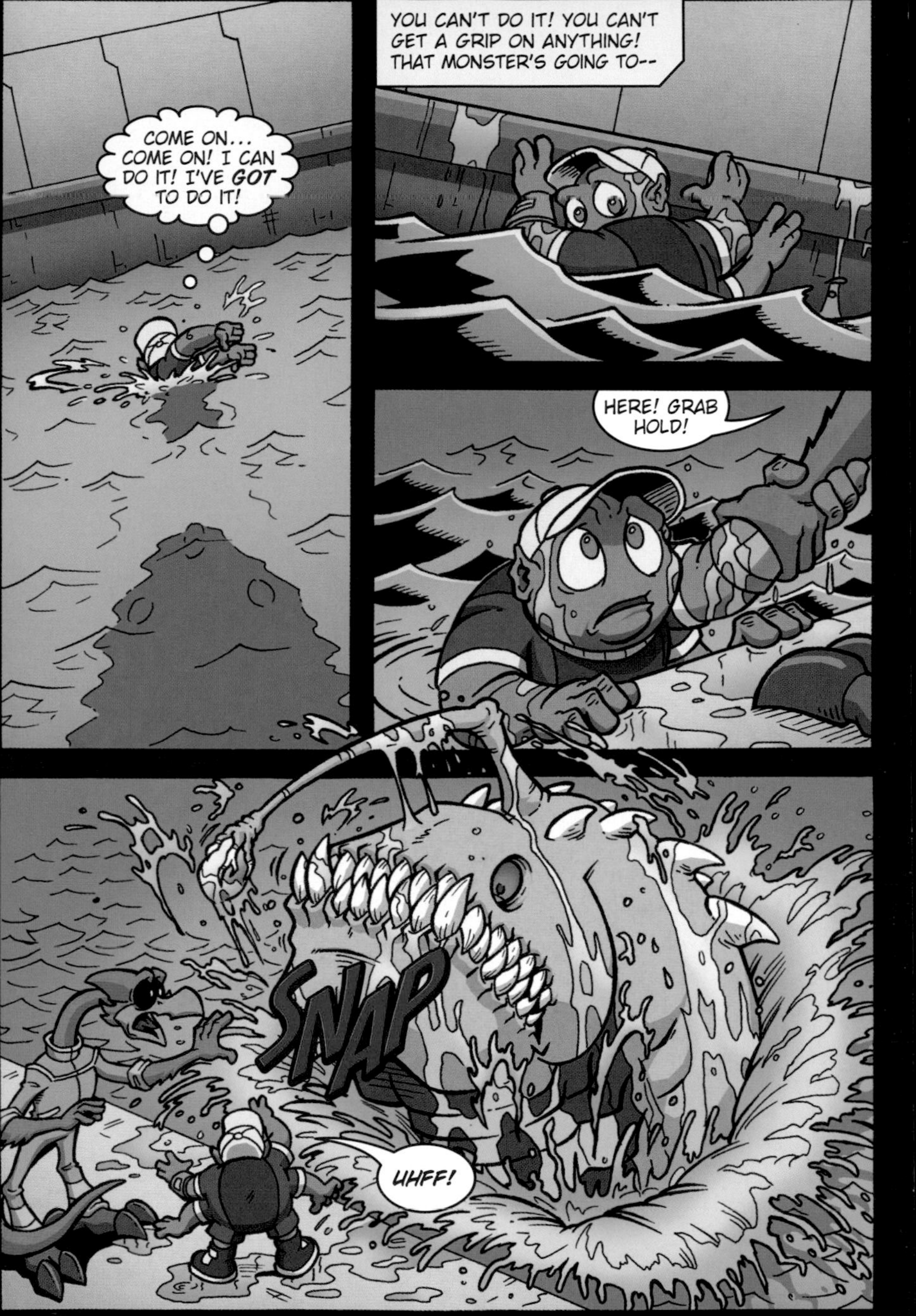
COME ON... COME ON! I CAN DO IT! I'VE GOT TO DO IT!
YOU CAN'T DO IT! YOU CAN'T GET A GRIP ON ANYTHING! THAT MONSTER'S GOING TO--
HERE! GRAB HOLD!
SNAP
UHFF!

GO ON TO THE NEXT PAGE.

You don't know who this Frongo is,
but he just saved your life!

WILL YOU . . .

. . . say "thanks" and ask him to call you a cab?
TURN TO PAGE 69.

. . . give him a big hug and invite him
to dinner with you and your mom?
TURN TO PAGE 77.

You head down the street past all the movie theaters. You guess these guys have never heard of a good old-fashioned Earth-style multiplex, huh? You get so distracted by all the different titles—stuff like *Tadpole Geniuses* and *The Man Who Ate 1,000 Flies*—that you almost walk right into a Zirifubi police officer.

The officer, whose name tag reads "Officer Biritti Milkstash," looks down her nose at you and then grins. "Let me guess," she says. "You're lost."

"You don't know the half of it!" You tell her about the explosions and getting stuck on the hover-bus.

"Well, let's get you back to the spaceport. Don't want you wandering around with all this danger in the city."

Once you're back, you thank Officer Milkstash and wave good-bye. You can find that wormhole analyzer somewhere else. You and your mom beat a hasty retreat from Planet J!

THE END

You spin around and dive, tackling the Frongo and taking you both out of harm's way. The Frongo groans and sits up as you get to your feet. "I say!" he exclaims. "You just saved my life!"

"Yeah, well, it was more than you were going to do for me," you respond angrily.

"No, no, no!" he cries. "There's been a misunderstanding! There was a deadly Zirifubian Octagon Spider on your back. I had to make you stand still while I brushed it off!"

Oh. Well. Now you feel kind of silly . . .

"Allow me to introduce myself. I am Mikipook Grungorsk, at your service. And since you saved my life, at great risk to your own, I would very much like to give you a reward. If you'll come with me . . ."

This guy *seems* sincere . . .
but he's also a complete stranger.

WILL YOU . . .

. . . go along to collect your reward?
TURN TO PAGE 70.

. . . thank him but politely leave?
TURN TO PAGE 94.

Alien or not, you can't just let a little tiny kid wander around like this! He (or she) might be just a *baby*. What if something bad happens, and you could have prevented it?

Carefully and slowly you step away from Honest Broknuk's shop and approach the little alien.

"Hey there," you say, as gently as possible. "Are you all right? Did you get lost?"

The child looks up at you helplessly and nods. "I don't know where Mommy and Daddy are!"

"Well, I can try to help you find them," you tell the kid. You're pretty sure it's a little boy. "Let me go see if I can call someone, and we'll—"

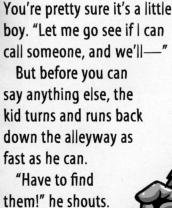

But before you can say anything else, the kid turns and runs back down the alleyway as fast as he can.

"Have to find them!" he shouts.

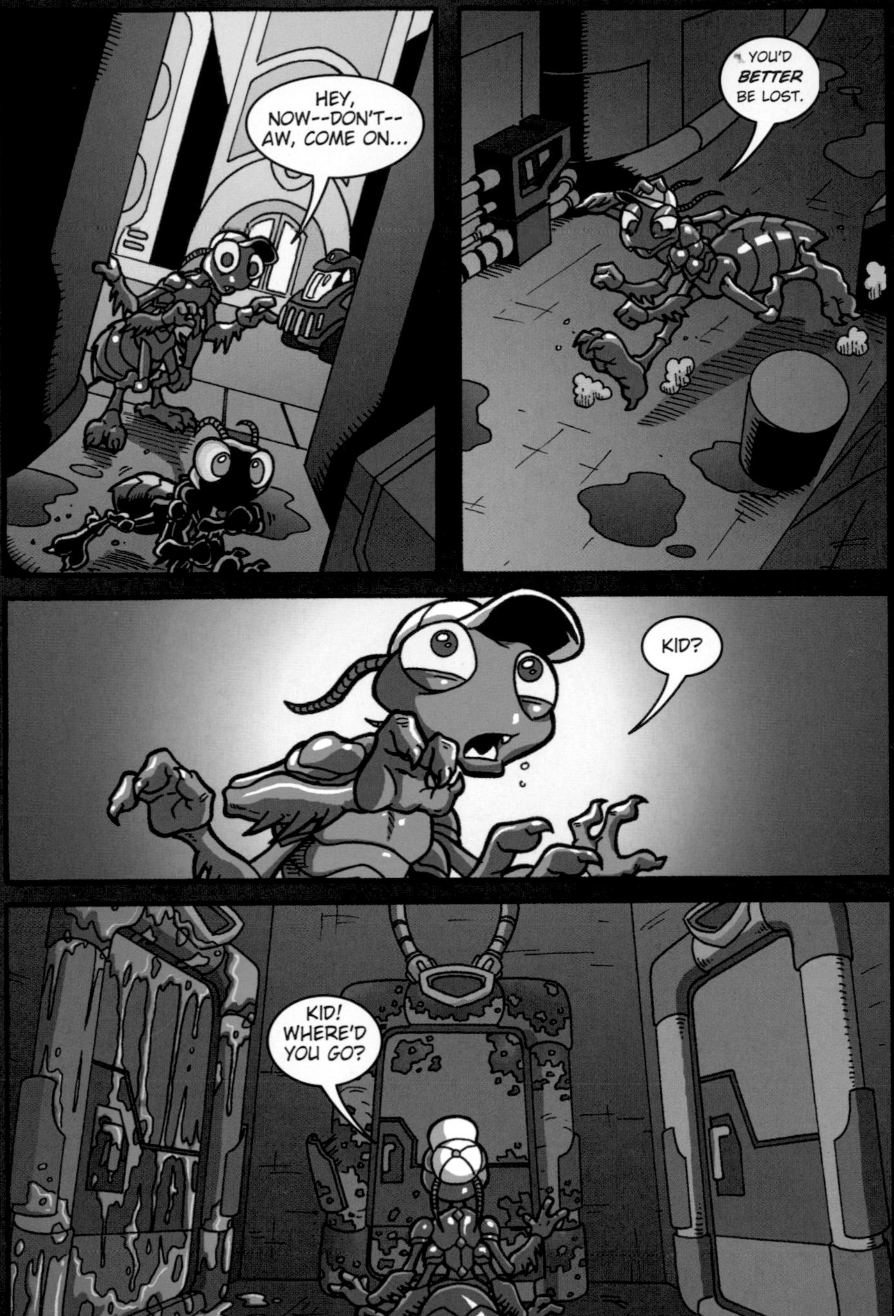
HEY, NOW--DON'T--AW, COME ON...
YOU'D BETTER BE LOST.
KID?
KID! WHERE'D YOU GO?

GO ON TO THE NEXT PAGE.

You've come too far to let
the kid just disappear now!

WILL YOU . . .

. . . try the slimy door on the left?
TURN TO PAGE 55.

. . . try the rusty one straight ahead?
TURN TO PAGE 62.

. . . go for the one on the right?
TURN TO PAGE 72.

Better not run. Who knows, that might get you shot. "Excuse me!" You raise your voice. "I'm human! I'm here by mistake!"

The vehicle stops, and a soldier pops up out of a roof hatch. "Human, you say? Prove it!"

Immediately you turn off your holo-projector and lower the hood on your jumpsuit. The soldier bellows an order. "Seize that human spy!"

Your head spins as you're grabbed and hauled off. Less than fifteen minutes later, you're floating in a weird zero-gravity holding cell. A Zirifubi general keeps asking the same question: "How long have you been working for the enemy?"

"I'm not a spy!" you tell him over and over. "I don't work for anybody! I'm just a kid!"

"Oh, I think you *are* a spy," he says. "And you're going to *stay* here until you admit it!"

You hope your mom isn't too worried. Because it looks like this is going to be a *long* wait.

THE END

You look around for some sort of public phone. *A-ha!* There's one. At least, you *think* that's a phone. It looks more like a giant seedpod planted on the street corner . . . but there's a keypad and a handset inside it, so you go over.

It's a phone, all right, but you quickly discover that you're not sure how to use it. There are three buttons at the top: one for fire, one for an ambulance, and one for the Zirifubi police. But the rest of the keypad is in Zirifubi—which looks like a bunch of chicken scratchings. You have no idea what button means what.

Just then a feathery hand clamps over your mouth! "Don't move," a voice whispers in your ear. You can see a reflection in the metal of the keypad: a weird-looking Frongo in a hooded sweatshirt has crept up and grabbed you!

GO ON TO THE NEXT PAGE.

You've only got a second to do something!

WILL YOU . . .

. . . hit the POLICE button on the keypad?
TURN TO PAGE 78.

. . . stomp the Frongo's foot as hard as you can and run?
TURN TO PAGE 64.

You want to try to get out of here and find the police
. . . but Kilippy's partner looks *very* nervous and he keeps
fingering his gun . . .

But you *have* to do it. The door is only ten feet away—
plus you think you can see a really big Makaknuk out
there, and he might be able to help—

You burst into a sprint, pushing past the Frongo
robbers. You hit the door with your shoulder, and it
springs open.

Both bandits start shouting *really* rude names at you,
and you hear a weird sound. You don't recognize it as
gunfire at first, but then you feel a blast of heat over your
head, and your baseball cap flies off. It's on *fire*.

"My hat!" you scream. But then . . .

GO ON TO THE NEXT PAGE.

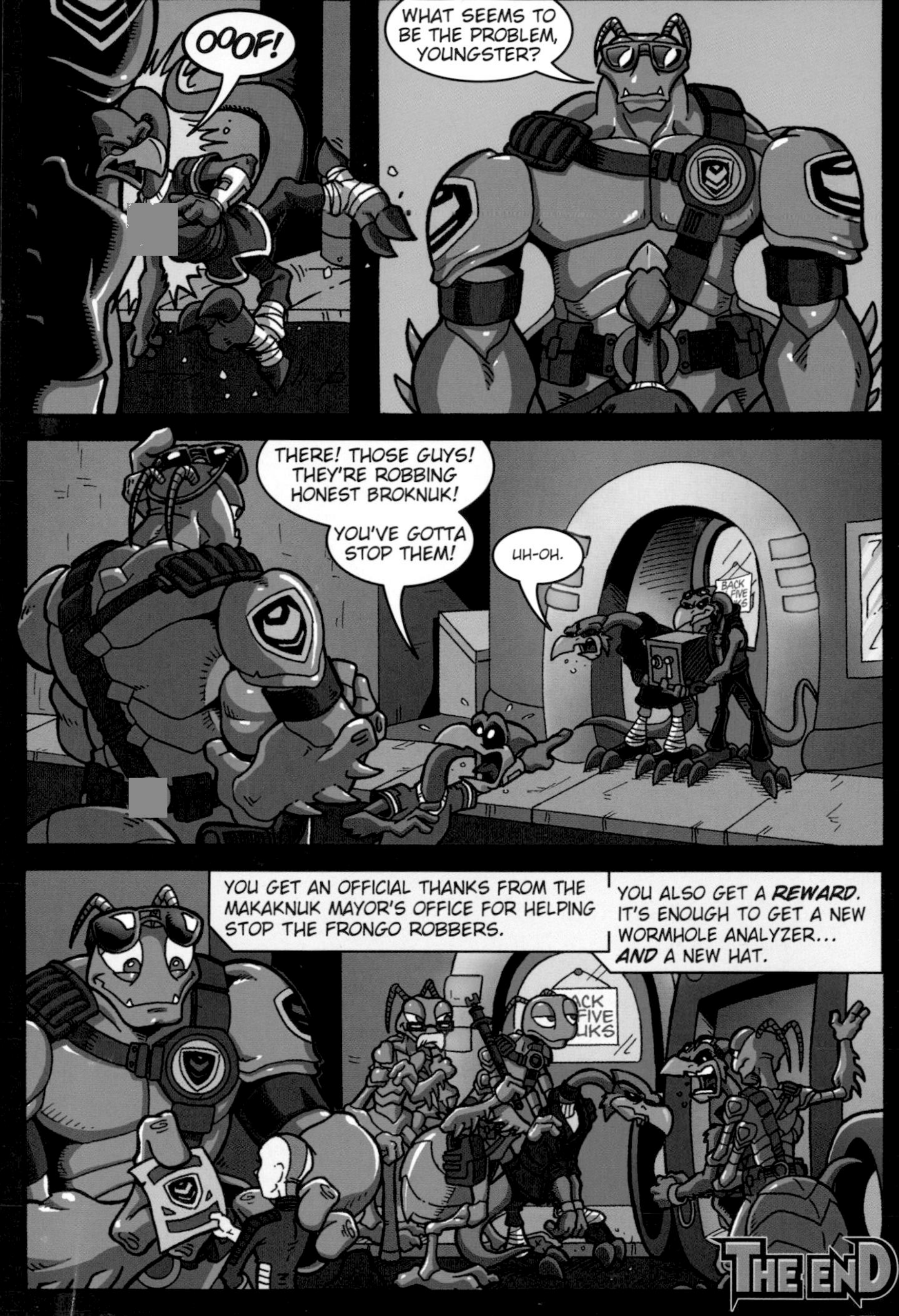
OOOF!
WHAT SEEMS TO BE THE PROBLEM, YOUNGSTER?
THERE! THOSE GUYS! THEY'RE ROBBING HONEST BROKNUK!
YOU'VE GOTTA STOP THEM!
UH-OH.
YOU GET AN OFFICIAL THANKS FROM THE MAKAKNUK MAYOR'S OFFICE FOR HELPING STOP THE FRONGO ROBBERS.
YOU ALSO GET A *REWARD*. IT'S ENOUGH TO GET A NEW WORMHOLE ANALYZER... *AND* A NEW HAT.
THE END

After five of the longest
minutes you've ever been
through, the shop door
opens. An elderly Makaknuk
wearing old-fashioned
reading glasses greets you.
"Come in, come in! I'm
Honest Broknuk! You've
obviously got some business
to do here!"

You start to tell him about
the little kid, but just then,
a couple of adult Makaknuks
come rushing up and scoop
the child into their arms.

"Oh, my baby!" the female
coos.

"How many times have we told you not to wander
off?" the father asks sternly.

The kid mumbles, "Sorry, Daddy."

Well, *that's* a relief. You won't have to get involved at
all. You follow Honest Broknuk inside.

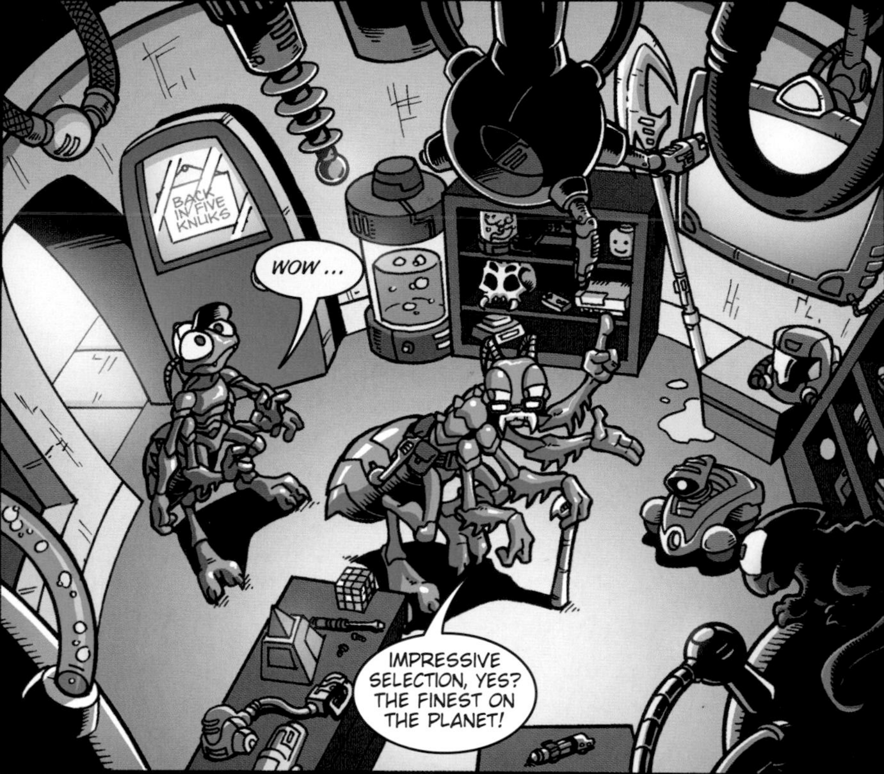
BACK IN FIVE KNUKS
WOW ...
IMPRESSIVE SELECTION, YES? THE FINEST ON THE PLANET!

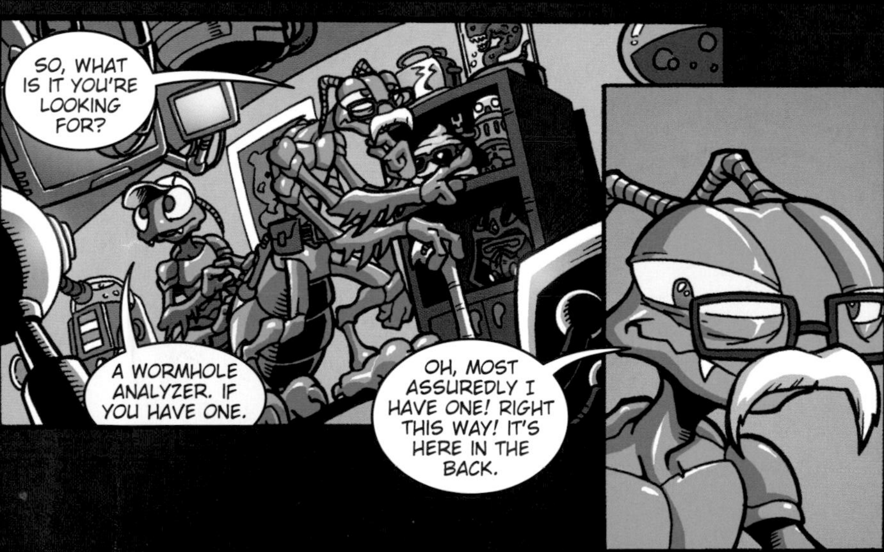
SO, WHAT IS IT YOU'RE LOOKING FOR?
A WORMHOLE ANALYZER. IF YOU HAVE ONE.
OH, MOST ASSUREDLY I HAVE ONE! RIGHT THIS WAY! IT'S HERE IN THE BACK.

Once you get to the back of the store, Honest Broknuk starts rummaging around on a dusty shelf. "I know I've got one here . . . a good one. I was saving it for an honest customer like yourself. Just wait here. I'll be back in a maknuk."

From the front room comes the sound of the door opening. "You've got more customers," you tell him. Then you hear running feet . . .

. . . and suddenly two nasty-looking Frongos dash right past you and go after Honest Broknuk, waving guns in the air! "All right, old man," they shout. "Open your safe! We know you've got money here. Give it to us!"

The two Frongo criminals didn't see you, but you can't get out of the store without being spotted. *Hey*, you think to yourself. *Maybe I can bluff my way out of this . . .*

GO ON TO THE NEXT PAGE.

With your holo-projector, you *could* disguise yourself as another Frongo . . . but you don't know if that would make any difference.

WILL YOU . . .

. . . stay disguised as a Makaknuk and take your chances?
TURN TO PAGE 88.

. . . switch your holo-projector to "Frongo"?
TURN TO PAGE 26.

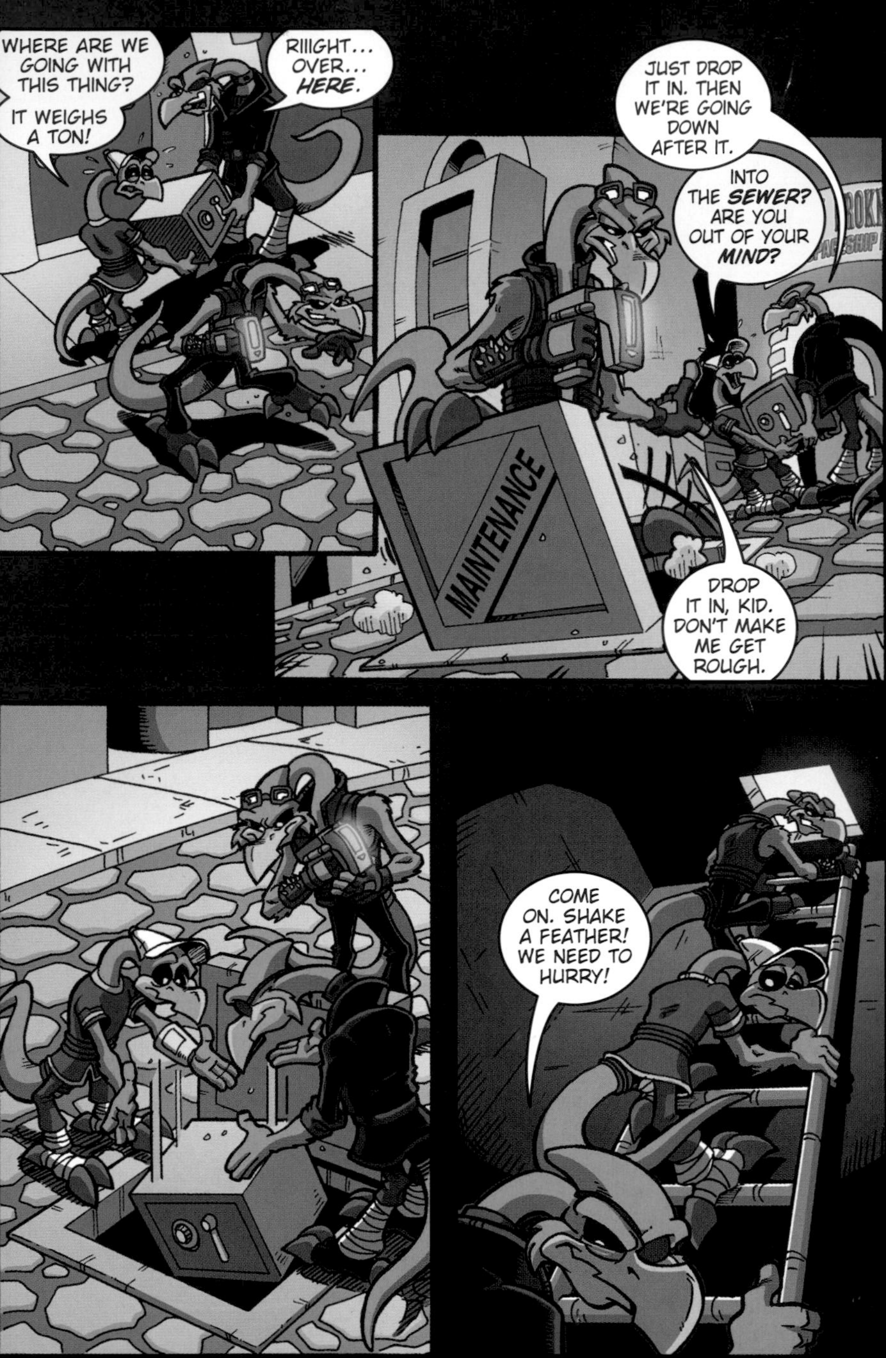
WHERE ARE WE GOING WITH THIS THING?
IT WEIGHS A TON!
RIIIGHT... OVER... HERE.
JUST DROP IT IN. THEN WE'RE GOING DOWN AFTER IT.
INTO THE SEWER? ARE YOU OUT OF YOUR MIND?
MAINTENANCE
DROP IT IN, KID. DON'T MAKE ME GET ROUGH.
COME ON. SHAKE A FEATHER! WE NEED TO HURRY!

Once all three of you are down in the sewers, the Frongo robbers heave the safe onto a little cart. Kilippy rolls the cart along in front, and you follow with his partner.

"So, uh . . . what's your name?" you ask the other Frongo.

"Markarlo. What's yours?"

Oh no! You should've known better! Now you've got to come up with something that sounds like a Frongo name. "Um . . . I'm Kitipitipat," you tell him.

You have *no* idea where that name came from.

"Pleased to meet you," Markarlo says. "It's always good to meet other soldiers in the revolution."

"Revolution?"

"Yeah! One day soon, the Frongo will take over this whole stinking planet. I can't wait!"

Just then you pass right below a big metal grate. You glance up—and there's your spaceship! You're walking right underneath it!

GO ON TO THE NEXT PAGE.

TWISTED JOURNEYS®

There's a remote-start control for the ship on your spare key ring! You could start the engines, and you *might* be able to escape in the confusion.

WILL YOU . . .

. . . take a chance with the engines and try to get away?
TURN TO PAGE 12.

. . . decide against such a long-shot idea and stay in the sewer for now?
TURN TO PAGE 60.

You push the left-hand door open and peer inside. It's pretty dark, but you can see a big, empty room . . . and there's the kid! He's over on the other side, still looking lost.

You step inside. "Hey, little guy! You shouldn't just run off like that. Come on, let me get you back to my mom. She'll know how to help."

Then you hear an adult's voice say, "No thanks, friend. I think I'm fine now." And you realize it's the kid talking! That's no *child*. That's just a short grown-up!

Then the door slams shut behind you, and you hear it lock. Huge, rough, insectile hands grab you in the darkness. "Hey!" you shout. "What's going on?"

"Just relax," a Makaknuk voice says in your ear, as you feel a needle sting your arm. This whole thing was a trap! "We're going to have you for dinner."

Then everything gets dark . . .

THE END

YOU FIGURE IF YOU JUST KEEP SWIMMING, YOU'LL GET TO SOME PLACE WHERE YOU CAN CLIMB OUT PRETTY EASILY.

OF COURSE, YOU COULD BE MISTAKEN...

GLUBB!

FILTRATION SUCCESSFUL. DISPOSING OF GARBAGE.

HEY!

The slide finally dumps you onto a wide conveyor belt. Garbage from all over the city is carried along on this thing. You immediately get to your feet and climb off of it.

But that leaves you—as you look around and take everything in—standing in the middle of a huge trash-disposal system. One thing is clear: The place where you're standing was *not* designed to be walked through!

Very slowly, and very carefully, you start making your way through a maze—no, more like a *jungle*—of machinery. You duck under whirling blades, twist sideways to avoid huge grinding gears, and jump over metal pistons that would break every bone in your body if they hit you. Surely there has to be an access tunnel or a catwalk or *something* . . .

And that's when you step on a loose panel and go crashing through the floor.

TURN TO PAGE 110.

THIS MAINTENANCE TUNNEL IS DEFINITELY THE WAY TO GO. IF THERE'S ANY MORE TROUBLE ON THE STREET, YOU'LL BE TOTALLY SAFE DOWN HERE.

THEY *ARE* SHOOTING! OR MAYBE THAT'S THE COPS. EITHER WAY, YOU DID THE RIGHT THING.

WELL...YOU *THINK* YOU DID THE RIGHT THING.

H-HELLO?

AAAAH!

58

TURN TO PAGE 68.

You go along with the robot as it drops Mikipook Grungorsk off at the nearest police station. Then the robot picks you up, sets you on its shoulder, and starts off down the street toward the spaceport.

"Thanks for saving my life," you tell it.

"Just doing my job," it replies in its mechanical voice. "That Frongo was more or less harmless, but you can't be too careful these days. There are rumors that a Frongo, a Zirifubi, and a Makaknuk are working together to take over the criminal underworld of Jarfarkarlarquillar."

"Well," you answer, "I'll be on the lookout for them, then."

"No," it says immediately. "My sensors can see through your holo-projector's disguise, and I have already called your mother at the spaceport. You and she are to take a wormhole analyzer and leave the planet at once. Your mere presence here might lead to further trouble."

That sounds good to you. As exciting as this planet is, you can't wait to leave!

THE END

You decide the engine idea is just too risky. So you follow Kilippy and Markarlo through the sewers . . . for a *long* time . . . and finally you emerge into a huge chamber filled with other rough-looking Frongo.

In the center of the chamber, there's a huge chair, kind of like a throne, made of thousands of little bits of scrap metal. In the chair sits the biggest, roughest-looking Frongo of the whole bunch. Kilippy takes you up to him.

"Who is this?" the big one asks. "I don't recognize the kid."

"Kitipitipat's okay," Kilippy says.

"We'll see about that!" the leader growls. "Santonlo! Come here!"

Another big, mean-looking Frongo walks over. The leader says, "You and Santonlo are going to fight, 'Kitipitipat.'"

Oh *no!*

GO ON TO THE NEXT PAGE.

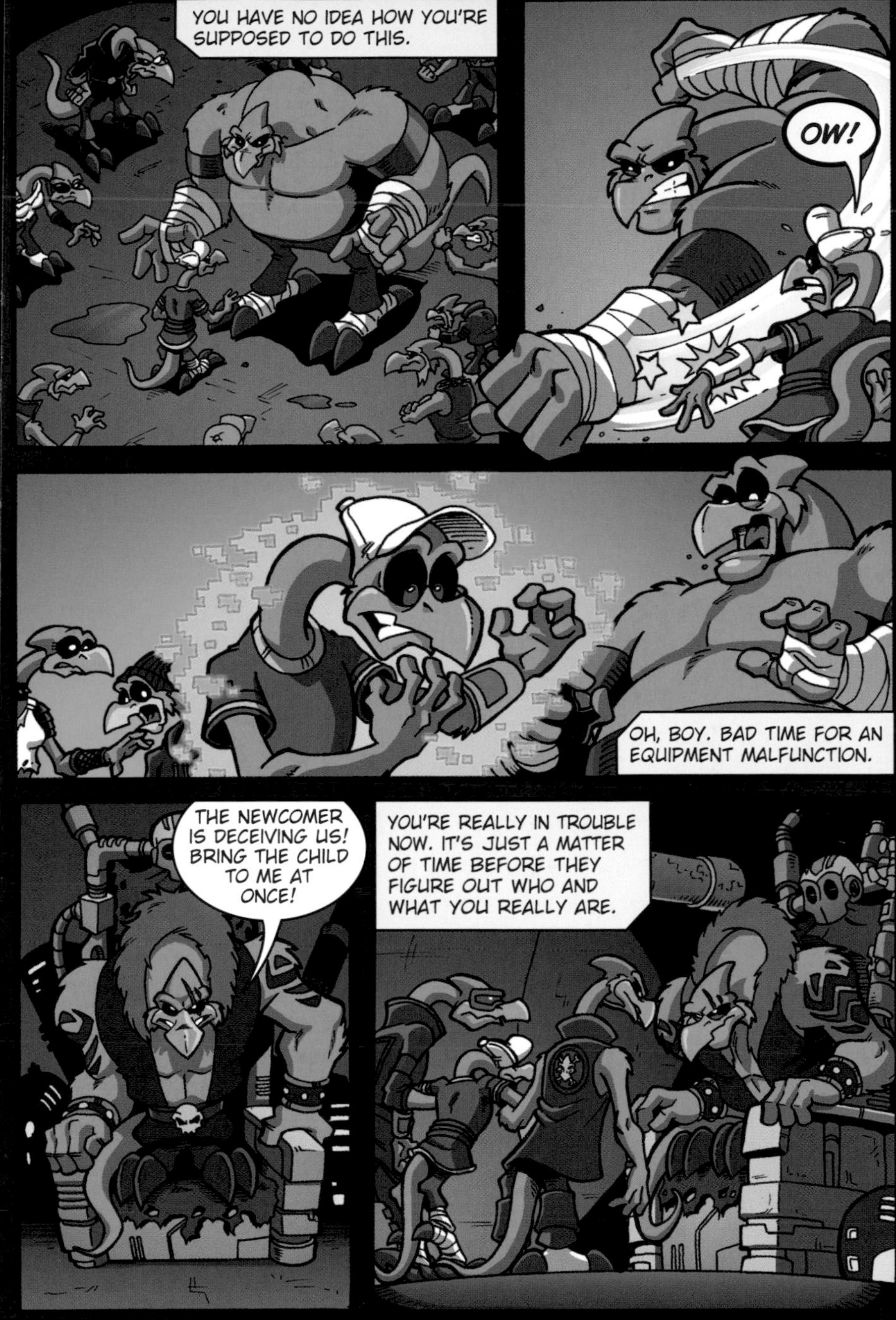

YOU HAVE NO IDEA HOW YOU'RE SUPPOSED TO DO THIS.
OW!
OH, BOY. BAD TIME FOR AN EQUIPMENT MALFUNCTION.
THE NEWCOMER IS DECEIVING US! BRING THE CHILD TO ME AT ONCE!
YOU'RE REALLY IN TROUBLE NOW. IT'S JUST A MATTER OF TIME BEFORE THEY FIGURE OUT WHO AND WHAT YOU REALLY ARE.

TURN TO PAGE 80.

The middle door swings open easily, and you find yourself in some kind of workshop.

It's filled with cool-looking alien technology that you don't recognize. But you can't get distracted. You're trying to find that kid!

There's a rattle from a doorway across from where you're standing. You make your way over to it . . .

. . . and there's the kid. But something's wrong with him. *Really* wrong—his head's on backward, and wires stick out of his neck! Then a brilliant flash of yellow light washes over you, and you can't move at all. The light *paralyzed* you.

"I see my little robotic decoy worked perfectly," an elderly Makaknuk says, moving out of the shadows. He's got a control device in one hand. "Lured in a nice healthy specimen! Well, it's off to the mines for you, child. Welcome to a new life of slavery!"

THE END

YOU'RE PRETTY SURE YOU'LL ONLY GET ONE SHOT AT EXPOSING THESE GUYS.

HOW CAN YOU MAKE THEM STAND OUT SO MUCH THAT THE COPS WILL HAVE NO CHOICE BUT TO STOP THEM?

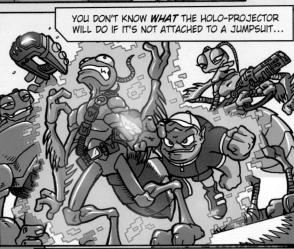

YOU DON'T KNOW *WHAT* THE HOLO-PROJECTOR WILL DO IF IT'S NOT ATTACHED TO A JUMPSUIT...

...BUT YOU KNOW IT'LL GET ATTENTION!

YOU'RE NOT SURE YOUR MOM IS GOING TO *BELIEVE* ALL THIS...BUT YOU'RE GOING TO HAVE A GREAT TIME TELLING HER!

THE END

As loud as you can, you shout, *"Let . . . me . . . go!"* and stomp down with everything you've got on the Frongo's foot.

The Frongo's scream is truly ear-piercing. Seriously. You think you might be deaf in that ear now.

But you're also free! While the Frongo hops around doing the One-Footed Dance of Pain, you sprint away from him to find the safest spot you can think of: right in the middle of a crowd. And look—there's a crowd, right across the street!

GO ON TO THE NEXT PAGE.

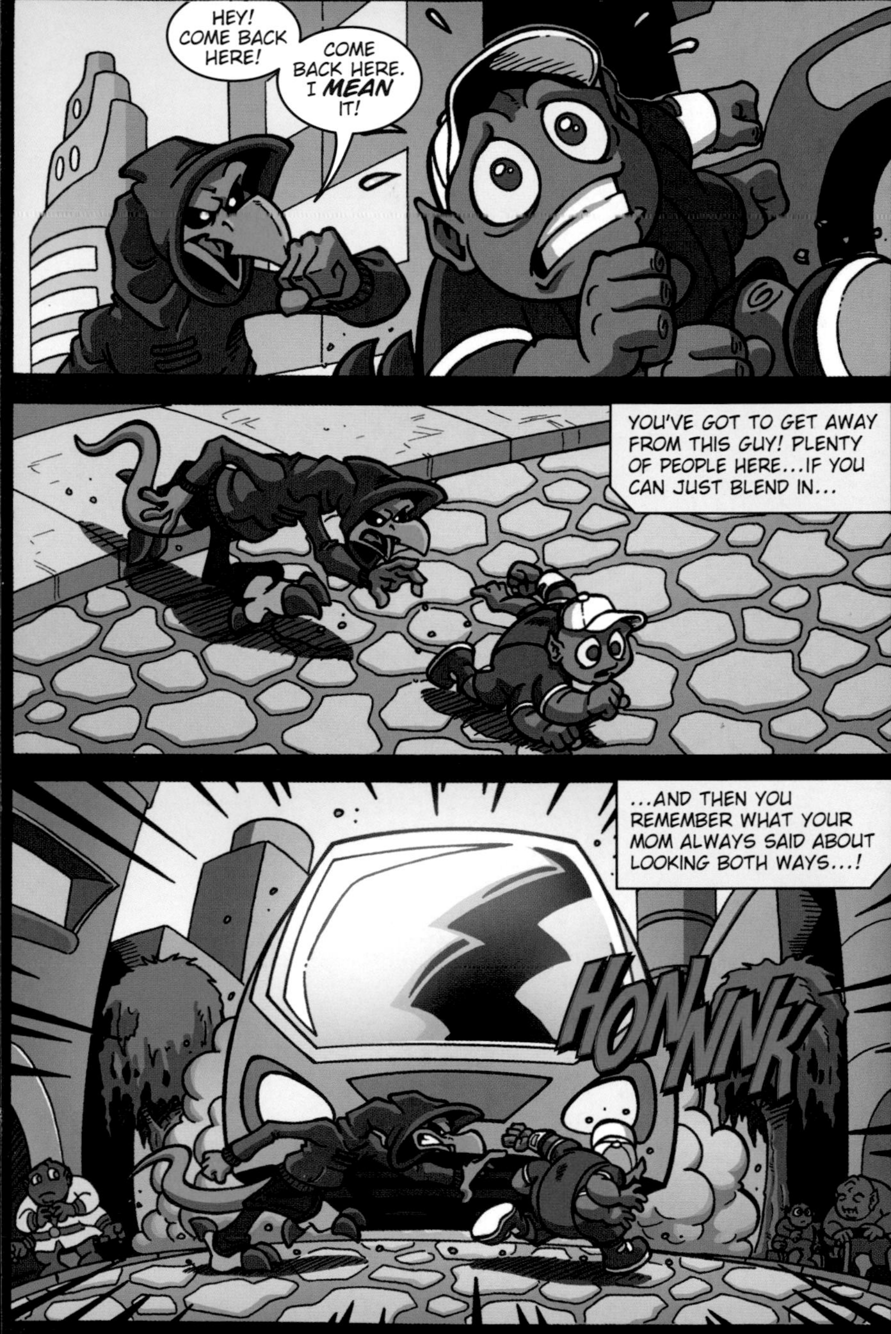
HEY! COME BACK HERE!
COME BACK HERE. I MEAN IT!
YOU'VE GOT TO GET AWAY FROM THIS GUY! PLENTY OF PEOPLE HERE...IF YOU CAN JUST BLEND IN...
...AND THEN YOU REMEMBER WHAT YOUR MOM ALWAYS SAID ABOUT LOOKING BOTH WAYS...!
HONNNK

The bus is almost on top of you!
You're sure you can get out of the way . . .
or you could spin around and pull the Frongo out
of the way, and the bus might miss you both.

WILL YOU . . .

. . . take a flying leap and save yourself?
TURN TO PAGE 91.

. . . try to get both you and the
alien out of harm's way?
TURN TO PAGE 38.

"Look, guys, you *really* want to let me go," you tell them, doing your best to sound convincing.

"And why is that?" the big one asks.

"I'm not really a Zirifubi! I'm a human kid! Plus I'm from off-planet. If you do anything to me, you won't just have the local cops after you. The Interplanetary Force will come down on you like a ton of bricks."

The Makaknuks take a moment to think about that.

Finally, they turn to you again. "You're right, this does change things," he says. "We can't risk you being found. So we're going to teleport you into our hive prison!"

And the last thing you see as a free human being is the flash from a teleportation globe. "Welcome to your new home!" the Makaknuk whispers, his voice echoing in your head. "You're never leaving!"

THE END

You're not alone down here!

WILL YOU . . .

. . . run away down the tunnel as fast as possible?
TURN TO PAGE 96.

. . . stand your ground and try to figure out whether you're really in danger?
TURN TO PAGE 81.

"Thanks, man," you say to the Frongo. "You just saved my bacon!"

He smiles. "I don't know what that means, but you're welcome. I saw you needed help, that's all."

"Well . . . I'm sort of lost. Do you think you could call me a cab?"

He laughs. "You're in luck. I *drive* a cab. Where do you want to go?"

You get back to the spaceport quickly and you give the cab driver a week's allowance for a tip. Your mother gives you a funny look as you scramble back on board.

"What are you doing?" your mother asks. "Don't you want to see any more of the planet?"

"No!" you shout, buckling in.

"But what about the part we need?" she asks. "Didn't you get one?"

"We can get the wormhole analyzer on the next planet! I'm not leaving this chair until we've taken off!"

And you don't.

THE END

"Reward me?" you ask, suspicious. You know better than to accept stuff from strangers. But then again, you did just save his life . . . so maybe he's not exactly a stranger? "Reward me how?"

"Why, I'll show you, right after I introduce you to my family! They're going to love the young Zirifubi who saved my life! Please, come with me!"

You *really* know better than to go anywhere with a stranger, but something about this guy makes you want to believe him. "And where exactly will we be going?"

"My apartment." He turns and points up at a building very close by. "Right up there. I live here in the Zirifubi section, because of my job. Come on, it's just a hop, skip, and jump! My wife and children will be there. Please?"

You look around. You guess it couldn't hurt to say hello to this guy's family. "All right!" you tell him, "I'll ask my mom."

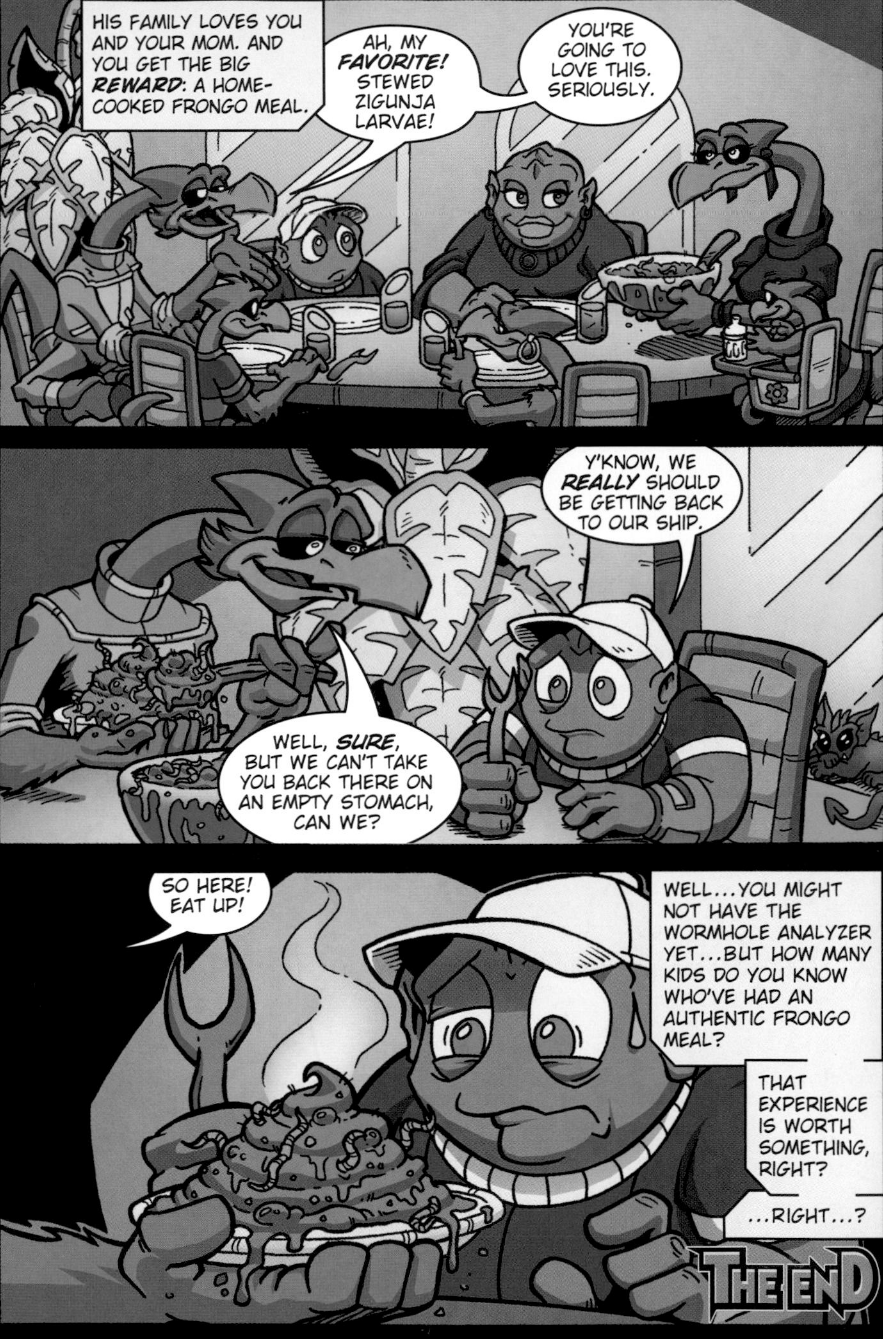
HIS FAMILY LOVES YOU AND YOUR MOM. AND YOU GET THE BIG REWARD: A HOME-COOKED FRONGO MEAL.
AH, MY FAVORITE! STEWED ZIGUNJA LARVAE!
YOU'RE GOING TO LOVE THIS. SERIOUSLY.
Y'KNOW, WE REALLY SHOULD BE GETTING BACK TO OUR SHIP.
WELL, SURE, BUT WE CAN'T TAKE YOU BACK THERE ON AN EMPTY STOMACH, CAN WE?
SO HERE! EAT UP!
WELL...YOU MIGHT NOT HAVE THE WORMHOLE ANALYZER YET...BUT HOW MANY KIDS DO YOU KNOW WHO'VE HAD AN AUTHENTIC FRONGO MEAL?
THAT EXPERIENCE IS WORTH SOMETHING, RIGHT?
...RIGHT...?
THE END

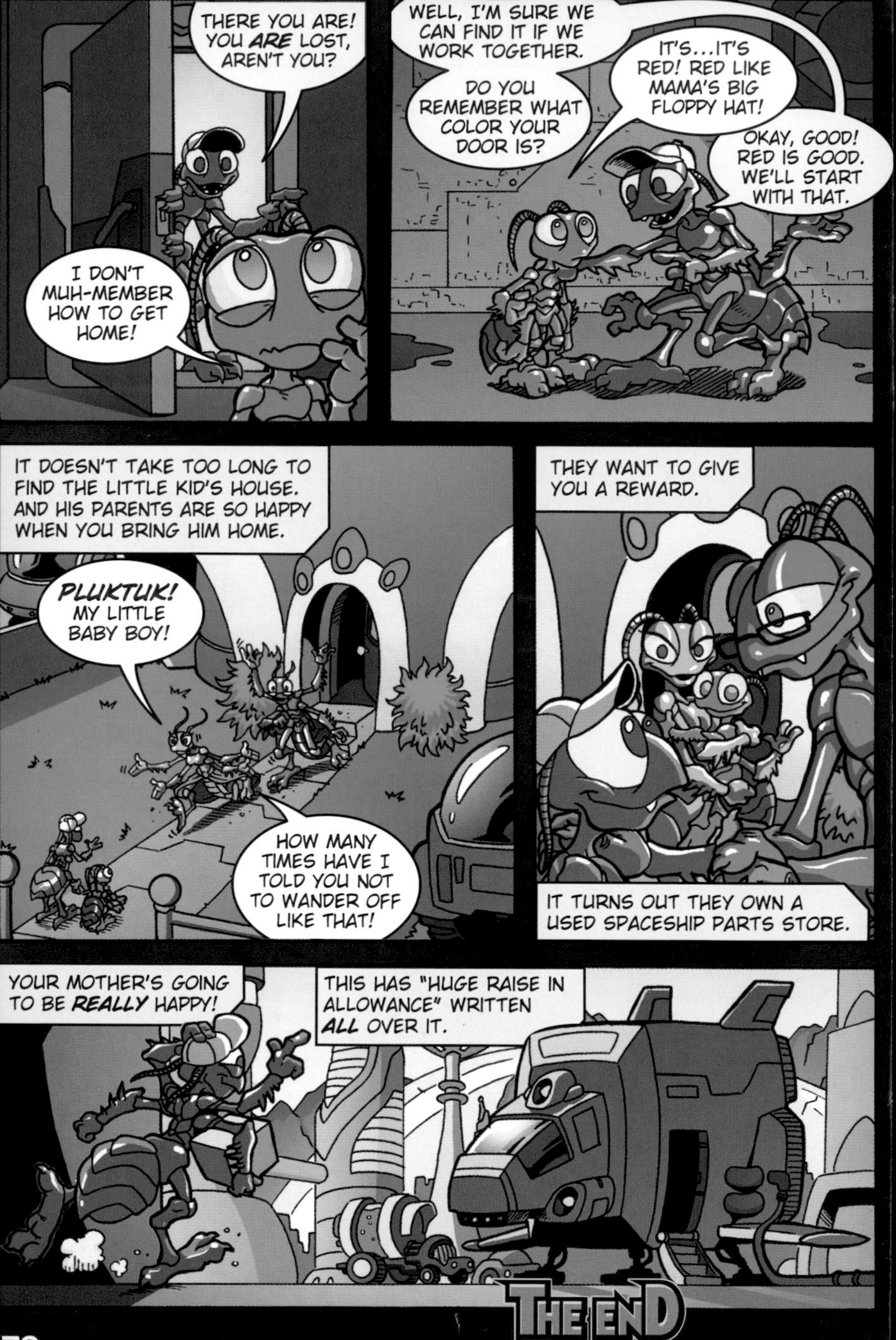
THERE YOU ARE! YOU ARE LOST, AREN'T YOU?
I DON'T MUH-MEMBER HOW TO GET HOME!
WELL, I'M SURE WE CAN FIND IT IF WE WORK TOGETHER.
DO YOU REMEMBER WHAT COLOR YOUR DOOR IS?
IT'S...IT'S RED! RED LIKE MAMA'S BIG FLOPPY HAT!
OKAY, GOOD! RED IS GOOD. WE'LL START WITH THAT.
IT DOESN'T TAKE TOO LONG TO FIND THE LITTLE KID'S HOUSE. AND HIS PARENTS ARE SO HAPPY WHEN YOU BRING HIM HOME.
PLUKTUK! MY LITTLE BABY BOY!
HOW MANY TIMES HAVE I TOLD YOU NOT TO WANDER OFF LIKE THAT!
THEY WANT TO GIVE YOU A REWARD.
IT TURNS OUT THEY OWN A USED SPACESHIP PARTS STORE.
YOUR MOTHER'S GOING TO BE REALLY HAPPY!
THIS HAS "HUGE RAISE IN ALLOWANCE" WRITTEN ALL OVER IT.
THE END

"Sir, you're right," you tell him. "I'm not what I appear. Let me show you."

You switch off your holo-projector and pull your hood down.

"Human?!" the leader splutters. For a second, you think he's going to kill you himself. But then he steps down from the scrap-metal throne and gives you the Frongo version of a big grin. "Why, we're delighted to have humans here on Jarfarkarlarquillar! Anything to build up the tourist trade, don't you know. Lots of Earth dollars!"

He walks you to an exit himself. "Just keep quiet about our little clubhouse down here, and we'll let you go. How's that sound?"

You're happy to promise your silence. Anything to get off this planet! Soon you're outside again and you make your way back to the ship. "I think we'll have the part *delivered*," your mom says, after you fill her in.

You think that's a *fantastic* idea.

THE END

You come to a stop in the loading dock of some really big building. The driver closes the loading-dock doors and leaves you alone.

Then silence.

It doesn't look like he's coming back any time soon, so you climb out and begin to look for a way to open the doors—and a thin, reedy voice calls out to you. "Oh, my! Oh, dear! Oh, my poor child, you must be *terrified!* Are you all right?"

The guy talking is a tall, thin, old *human* wearing a white lab coat. He walks toward you, carrying a clipboard and a really fancy pen. "I can't believe he did it again! My android, Giorgio—his programming is getting faulty. I really must retire him. Listen, you have my most sincere apologies for this. I'm really quite embarrassed."

"Who are you?" you ask. "Where am I?"

"Again, I apologize," he says. "I am Dr. Terawatt Sprigmarsh."

GO ON TO THE NEXT PAGE.

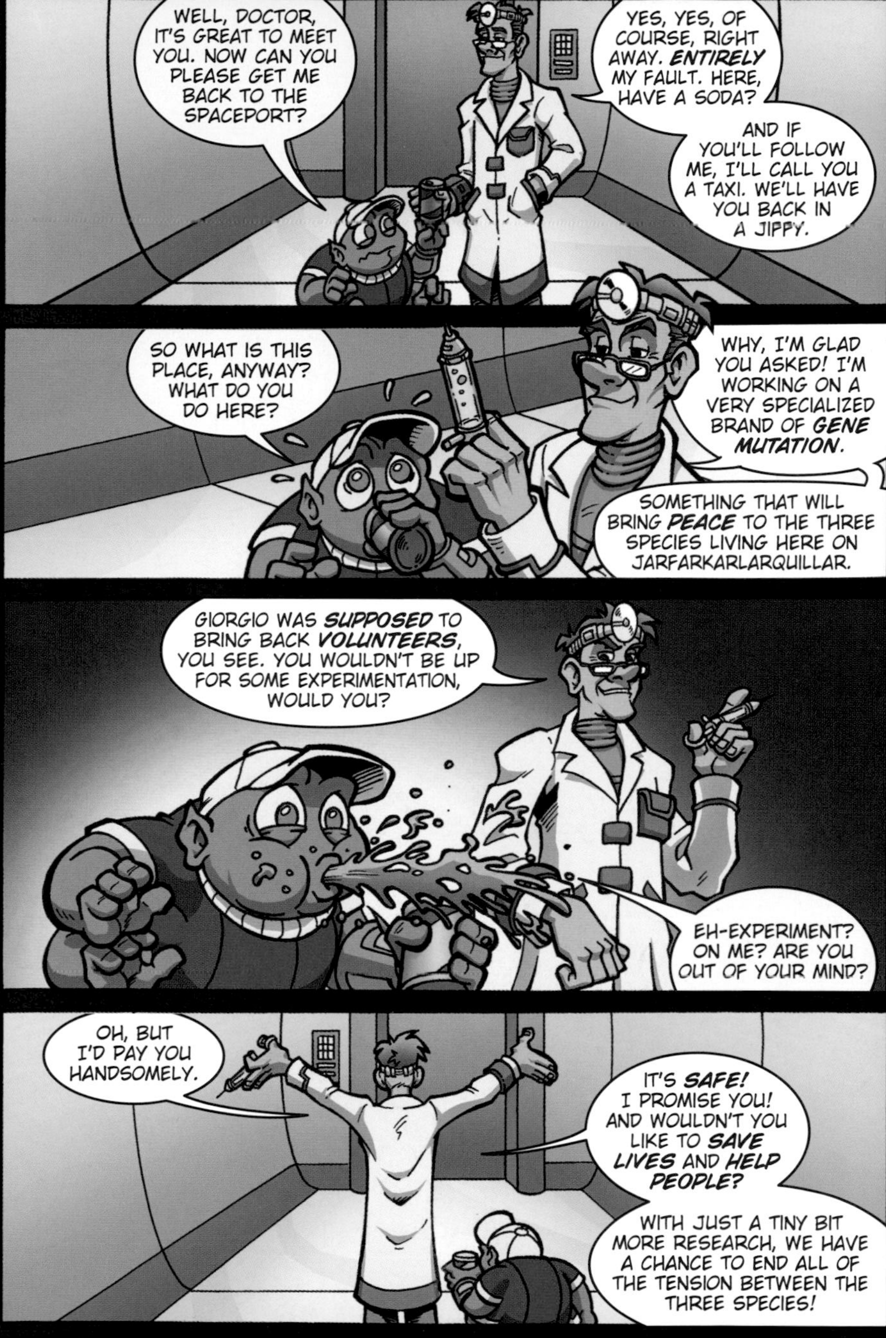
WELL, DOCTOR, IT'S GREAT TO MEET YOU. NOW CAN YOU PLEASE GET ME BACK TO THE SPACEPORT?
YES, YES, OF COURSE, RIGHT AWAY. ENTIRELY MY FAULT. HERE, HAVE A SODA?
AND IF YOU'LL FOLLOW ME, I'LL CALL YOU A TAXI. WE'LL HAVE YOU BACK IN A JIFFY.
SO WHAT IS THIS PLACE, ANYWAY? WHAT DO YOU DO HERE?
WHY, I'M GLAD YOU ASKED! I'M WORKING ON A VERY SPECIALIZED BRAND OF GENE MUTATION.
SOMETHING THAT WILL BRING PEACE TO THE THREE SPECIES LIVING HERE ON JARFARKARLARQUILLAR.
GIORGIO WAS SUPPOSED TO BRING BACK VOLUNTEERS, YOU SEE. YOU WOULDN'T BE UP FOR SOME EXPERIMENTATION, WOULD YOU?
EH-EXPERIMENT? ON ME? ARE YOU OUT OF YOUR MIND?
OH, BUT I'D PAY YOU HANDSOMELY.
IT'S SAFE! I PROMISE YOU! AND WOULDN'T YOU LIKE TO SAVE LIVES AND HELP PEOPLE?
WITH JUST A TINY BIT MORE RESEARCH, WE HAVE A CHANCE TO END ALL OF THE TENSION BETWEEN THE THREE SPECIES!

GO ON TO THE NEXT PAGE.

It *would* be nice to have some spending money
. . . of course, this guy strikes you as pretty crazy too.

WILL YOU . . .

. . . agree to the test,
since he promised it would be safe?
TURN TO PAGE 98.

. . . forget about waiting for a cab
and just run away?
TURN TO PAGE 33.

. . . grab the needle from him
so you can turn it over to the police?
TURN TO PAGE 105.

"That was *amazing*," you say. "Thank you! Listen, I don't know that my mom and I can give you much in return, but at least let us buy you a meal."

The Frongo smiles. "I'd be honored."

The Frongo's name is Vrosco. You take him back to the spaceport and introduce him to your mom—and then the most amazing thing happens.

A Makaknuk reporter overhears you talking and ends up joining the three of you for dinner. She interviews Vrosco there and immediately puts out a news story: FRONGO SAVES ZIRIFUBI CHILD'S LIFE. It turns into a planetwide news event! Suddenly the three alien species see that there aren't that many differences between them after all. Vrosco saving your life has brought peace to Planet J.

Now, if you and your mom can just get away before anybody realizes you're *not* a Zirifubi . . .

THE END

You can't get away and you can't turn around, but your right hand is still free. Quick as lightning, you reach up and punch the button with the symbol for the police.

Then something happens that you never expected: The entire seedpod splits apart and *starts unfolding*. Within seconds it has become a big, bizarre robot, with the symbol for the Zirifubi police on its chest!

"Wait!" the Frongo shouts. "This was all a big misunderstanding! The kid had a big spider on his back! I wasn't trying to hurt him!"

The robot focuses its one big, yellow eye on the Frongo. **"IDENTIFICATION POSITIVE,"** it says. **"MIKIPOOK GRUNGORSK. 8176 NOSEDIVE LANE. WANTED FOR SIXTEEN OUTSTANDING PARKING TICKETS."**

The Frongo backs away, afraid. "No way! *No way!*"

GO ON TO THE NEXT PAGE.

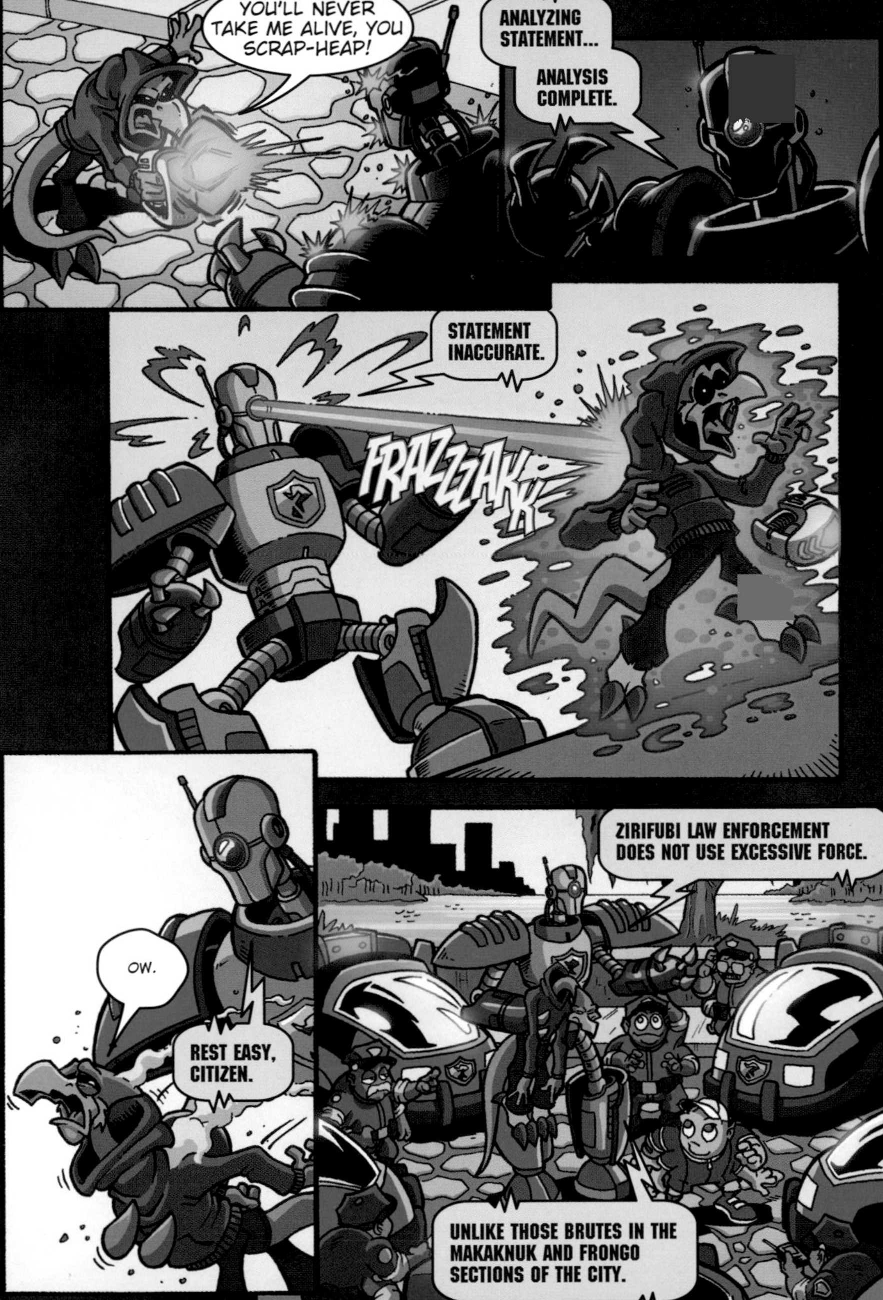
YOU'LL NEVER TAKE ME ALIVE, YOU SCRAP-HEAP!
ANALYZING STATEMENT...
ANALYSIS COMPLETE.
STATEMENT INACCURATE.
FRAZZZAKK
OW.
REST EASY, CITIZEN.
ZIRIFUBI LAW ENFORCEMENT DOES NOT USE EXCESSIVE FORCE.
UNLIKE THOSE BRUTES IN THE MAKAKNUK AND FRONGO SECTIONS OF THE CITY.

Choice after choice runs through your head.

WILL YOU . . .

. . . turn the holo-projector off and reveal yourself as human?
TURN TO PAGE 73.

. . . switch to Zirifubi and try to bluff your way out?
TURN TO PAGE 22.

. . . become a Makaknuk to try to confuse them?
TURN TO PAGE 11.

. . . stay disguised as a Frongo and convince them that nothing's out of the ordinary?
TURN TO PAGE 87.

Cautiously you take a step toward the big, glinting eyes. "Um . . . hi? You guys, uh . . . come here often?"

Before you can even kick yourself for how lame that sounded, three dangerous-looking Makaknuks step out into the light. "Only when we're robbing Zirifubi banks," the biggest one says.

You get a cold feeling in the pit of your stomach. "You guys are bank robbers *too*?"

The big Makaknuk shrugs. "We're bank robber robbers, technically. We were just about to attack the chumps who pulled that job up on the street and take their loot. But then you showed up." The other two circle and surround you. "I guess you'll have to be *another* diversion, yes?"

GO ON TO THE NEXT PAGE.

It's obvious you're in pretty deep at this point.

WILL YOU . . .

. . . argue with the bank robbers about
why you *shouldn't* be a diversion?
TURN TO PAGE 67.

. . . cooperate and wait for a chance
to do something else?
TURN TO PAGE 63.

All right. So you're changing? Let's see how far you can take this.

First, the legs. Your skin gets harder, like a shell . . . like Makaknuk legs! Your arms and torso ripple and grow feathers. They're like Frongo feathers! That just leaves your head, which twitches and warps and turns into a *real* Zirifubi head.

You're like all three of the Planet J alien species, rolled into one—and it feels kind of *good*. You feel strong, and fast, and . . . it's so weird, it's cool!

"Success!" shouts Dr. Sprigmarsh. "Success beyond my wildest dreams! Don't you see, my child? As all three species combined, you'll be a symbol of peace! Come, come with me! We must tell the world! You'll be a *hero!*"

Hero, huh? You like the sound of that. A chance to help the whole planet? That's a little more important than getting to Granddad's on time.

THE END

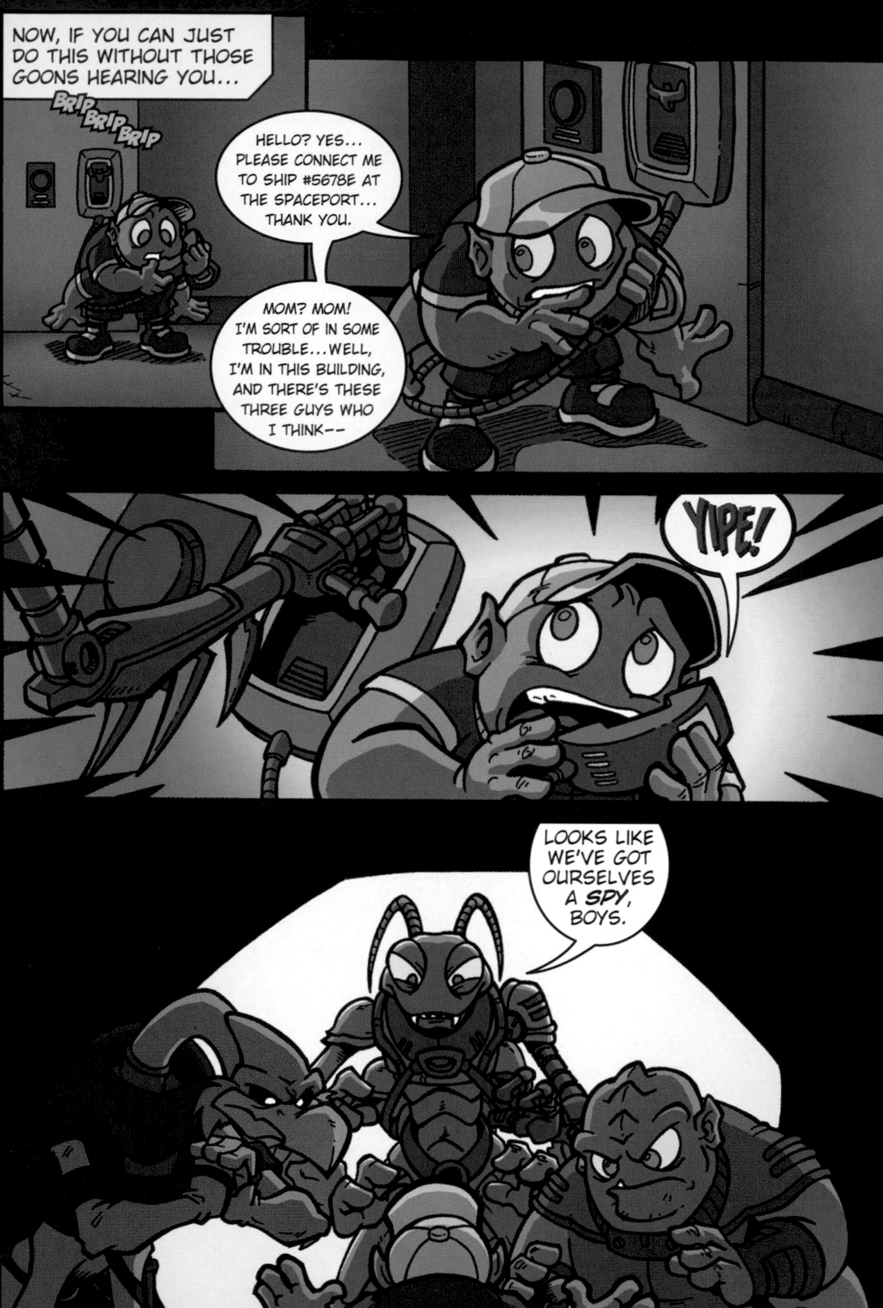
NOW, IF YOU CAN JUST DO THIS WITHOUT THOSE GOONS HEARING YOU...
BRIP BRIP BRIP
HELLO? YES... PLEASE CONNECT ME TO SHIP #5678E AT THE SPACEPORT... THANK YOU.
MOM? MOM! I'M SORT OF IN SOME TROUBLE...WELL, I'M IN THIS BUILDING, AND THERE'S THESE THREE GUYS WHO I THINK--
YIPE!
LOOKS LIKE WE'VE GOT OURSELVES A SPY, BOYS.

GO ON TO THE NEXT PAGE.

The Frongo and the Zirifubi grab your arms, haul you back into the room with the table and chairs, and tie you up.

"What do you think we should do with the spy?" the Frongo asks.

"Well, you know me," the Makaknuk growls. "I'm always up for some spy soup."

But that starts a *huge* fight among the criminals about Zirifubi not eating other Zirifubi . . . and then suddenly the door bursts open! A dozen heavily armed Zirifubi police officers swarm into the place, and in a flash, all three criminals are in handcuffs.

One of the Zirifubi cops unties you. "Thank goodness you guys showed up!" you tell him. "I was about to be lunch!"

"Yeah, well, we couldn't have found the place if you hadn't made that phone call. Good job, kid. You'll probably get a reward for this."

You haven't even started thinking about your reward money when you hear a familiar voice.

"There you are! Are you all right?"

You turn around to see your mom rushing toward you, and then she grabs you off your feet and spins you around in a huge hug. "Oh, my sweet baby! I was so *worried!*"

As you're spinning around, you notice all the Zirifubi cops staring at you. Someone snickers.

Aargh! "Mom, *please!* You're embarrassing me!"

She finally puts you down. "Well, I was worried," she says again. Then she takes your hand. "Come on. We're going back to the ship. You're getting some hot cocoa."

"But, *Mom . . . !*"

"No arguing! Come on. Now!"

Actually . . . laughing cops or not, some hot cocoa does sound nice.

THE END

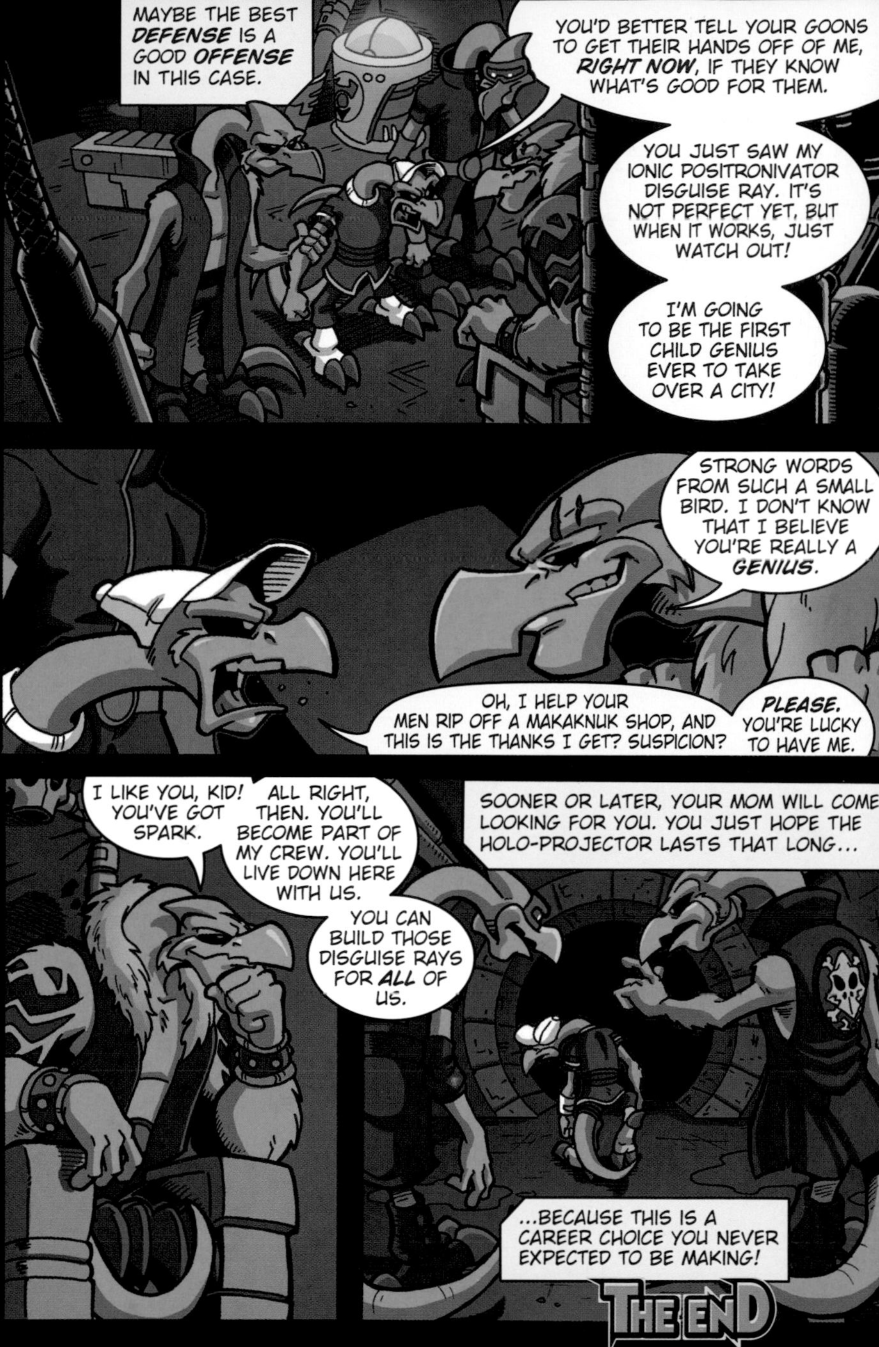
MAYBE THE BEST DEFENSE IS A GOOD OFFENSE IN THIS CASE.
YOU'D BETTER TELL YOUR GOONS TO GET THEIR HANDS OFF OF ME, RIGHT NOW, IF THEY KNOW WHAT'S GOOD FOR THEM.
YOU JUST SAW MY IONIC POSITRONIVATOR DISGUISE RAY. IT'S NOT PERFECT YET, BUT WHEN IT WORKS, JUST WATCH OUT!
I'M GOING TO BE THE FIRST CHILD GENIUS EVER TO TAKE OVER A CITY!
STRONG WORDS FROM SUCH A SMALL BIRD. I DON'T KNOW THAT I BELIEVE YOU'RE REALLY A GENIUS.
OH, I HELP YOUR MEN RIP OFF A MAKAKNUK SHOP, AND THIS IS THE THANKS I GET? SUSPICION?
PLEASE. YOU'RE LUCKY TO HAVE ME.
I LIKE YOU, KID! YOU'VE GOT SPARK.
ALL RIGHT, THEN. YOU'LL BECOME PART OF MY CREW. YOU'LL LIVE DOWN HERE WITH US.
YOU CAN BUILD THOSE DISGUISE RAYS FOR ALL OF US.
SOONER OR LATER, YOUR MOM WILL COME LOOKING FOR YOU. YOU JUST HOPE THE HOLO-PROJECTOR LASTS THAT LONG...
...BECAUSE THIS IS A CAREER CHOICE YOU NEVER EXPECTED TO BE MAKING!
THE END

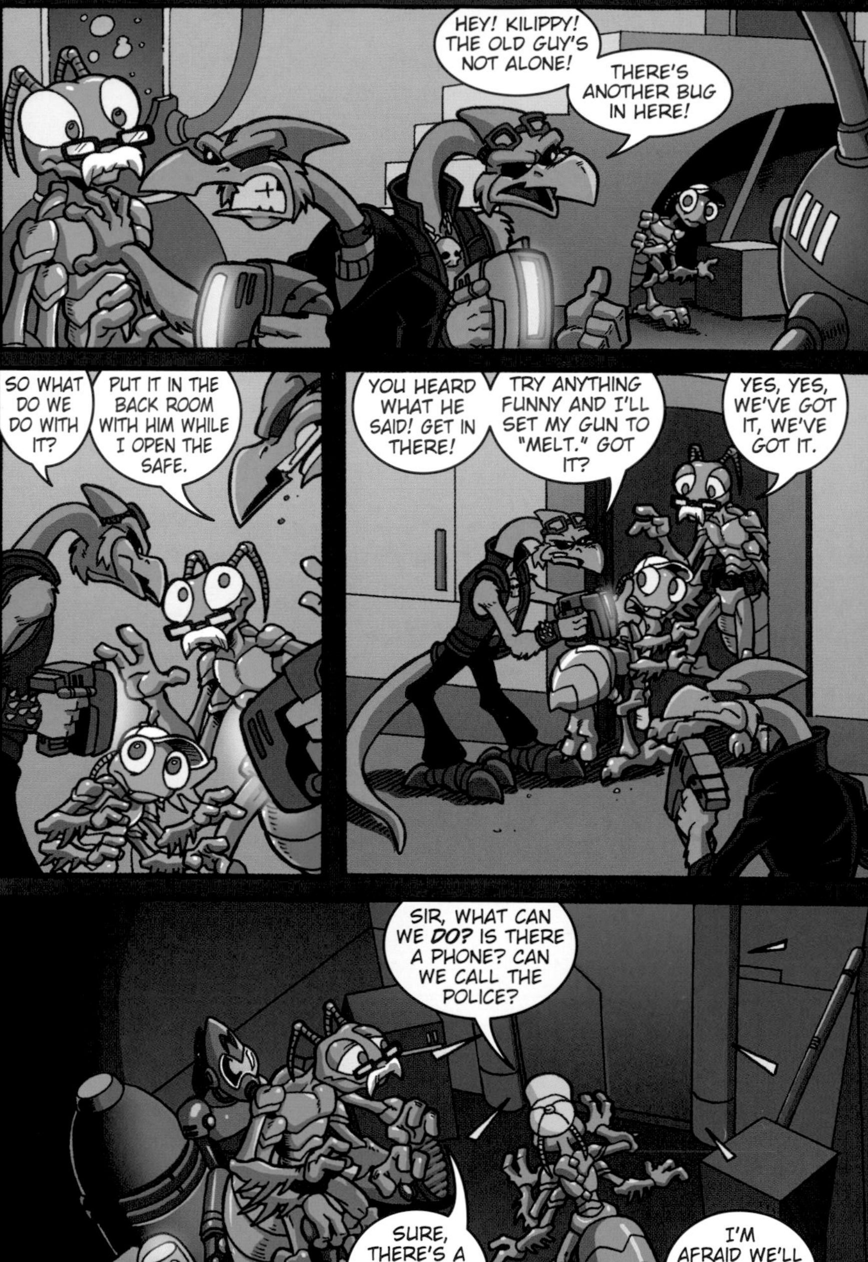
HEY! KILIPPY! THE OLD GUY'S NOT ALONE!
THERE'S ANOTHER BUG IN HERE!
SO WHAT DO WE DO WITH IT?
PUT IT IN THE BACK ROOM WITH HIM WHILE I OPEN THE SAFE.
YOU HEARD WHAT HE SAID! GET IN THERE!
TRY ANYTHING FUNNY AND I'LL SET MY GUN TO "MELT." GOT IT?
YES, YES, WE'VE GOT IT, WE'VE GOT IT.
SIR, WHAT CAN WE *DO?* IS THERE A PHONE? CAN WE CALL THE POLICE?
SURE, THERE'S A PHONE. OUT THERE WITH THEM.
I'M AFRAID WE'LL BE SITTING TIGHT FOR A WHILE.

GO ON TO THE NEXT PAGE.

You get the feeling Honest Broknuk should be a lot more worried than he appears to be.

"You're taking this *awfully* well," you say. "Shouldn't you be more concerned? Aren't our *lives* in danger?"

Honest Broknuk shrugs. "I don't think so. This kind of thing happens all the time. Ever since this city was built, the Frongo have been running over here, stealing a few things, then running back. They're hard to catch with those long legs, you know!"

"So you *let* this go on?"

"Usually. They rarely take anything truly valuable. I mean, I've only got ten credits in the safe. If we just sit tight, everything will be fine." He pauses. "Unless, of course, they take your wormhole analyzer. Those things are hard to come by. I'm not sure any other vendor on the planet has one."

So if you just hang out back here you'll be safe . . . but those criminals *might* take the part you need for your spaceship.

WILL YOU . . .

. . . play it safe, stay put, and cooperate?
TURN TO PAGE 95.

. . . go out and make sure they don't take the wormhole analyzer?
TURN TO PAGE 106.

You take a running jump and dive out of the way, just as the bus hits the Frongo and flattens him.

Someone in the crowd says, "I can't believe you did that."

Before you can react, someone else says, "You had a chance to save that guy, and you didn't! That was *horrible!*"

Before you know it, a Zirifubi cop named Officer Milkstash has you in handcuffs and leads you off to face the Municipal Court. "That was Mikipook Grungorsk. Good guy. I knew him. And he wasn't chasing you for no reason. You had a big spider on your back."

Wow. . .you feel lower than dirt. Whatever punishment they give you, you figure you probably deserve it.

THE END

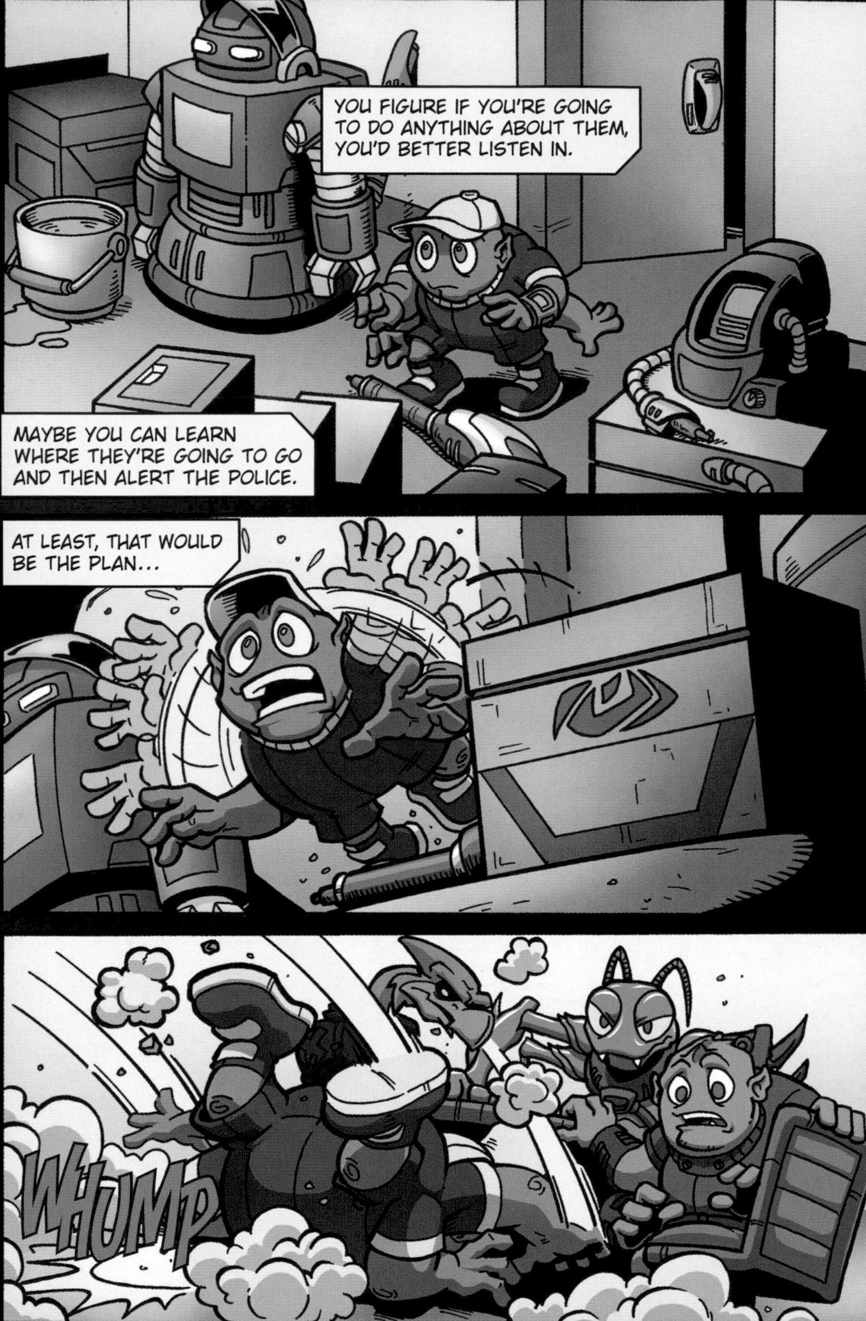

YOU FIGURE IF YOU'RE GOING TO DO ANYTHING ABOUT THEM, YOU'D BETTER LISTEN IN.
MAYBE YOU CAN LEARN WHERE THEY'RE GOING TO GO AND THEN ALERT THE POLICE.
AT LEAST, THAT WOULD BE THE PLAN...
WHUMP

GO ON TO THE NEXT PAGE.

"Well, look what just fell into our laps," the big Makaknuk says. "A spy!"

"Wait, wait, no, hold on," you say, scrambling to your feet. The Frongo and the Zirifubi have already come around and surrounded you. "I was almost kidnapped, and I jumped out of this thing, and I ended up here! I'm no spy! Look!" You switch off your disguise. "I'm not even a Zirifubi! I'm a human kid! My mom and I just stopped here to get a part for our ship!"

The Makaknuk's eyes suddenly gleam. "You're . . . *human*. All *right* then."

". . . Pardon me?" you say nervously.

He grabs you around the throat with one huge hand. "A Zirifubi spy is one thing. But making an example out of an interfering alien? That'll stir up so much trouble you wouldn't *believe* it."

Then you see the gun in his other hand. Man . . . you really should've stayed in that storeroom!

THE END

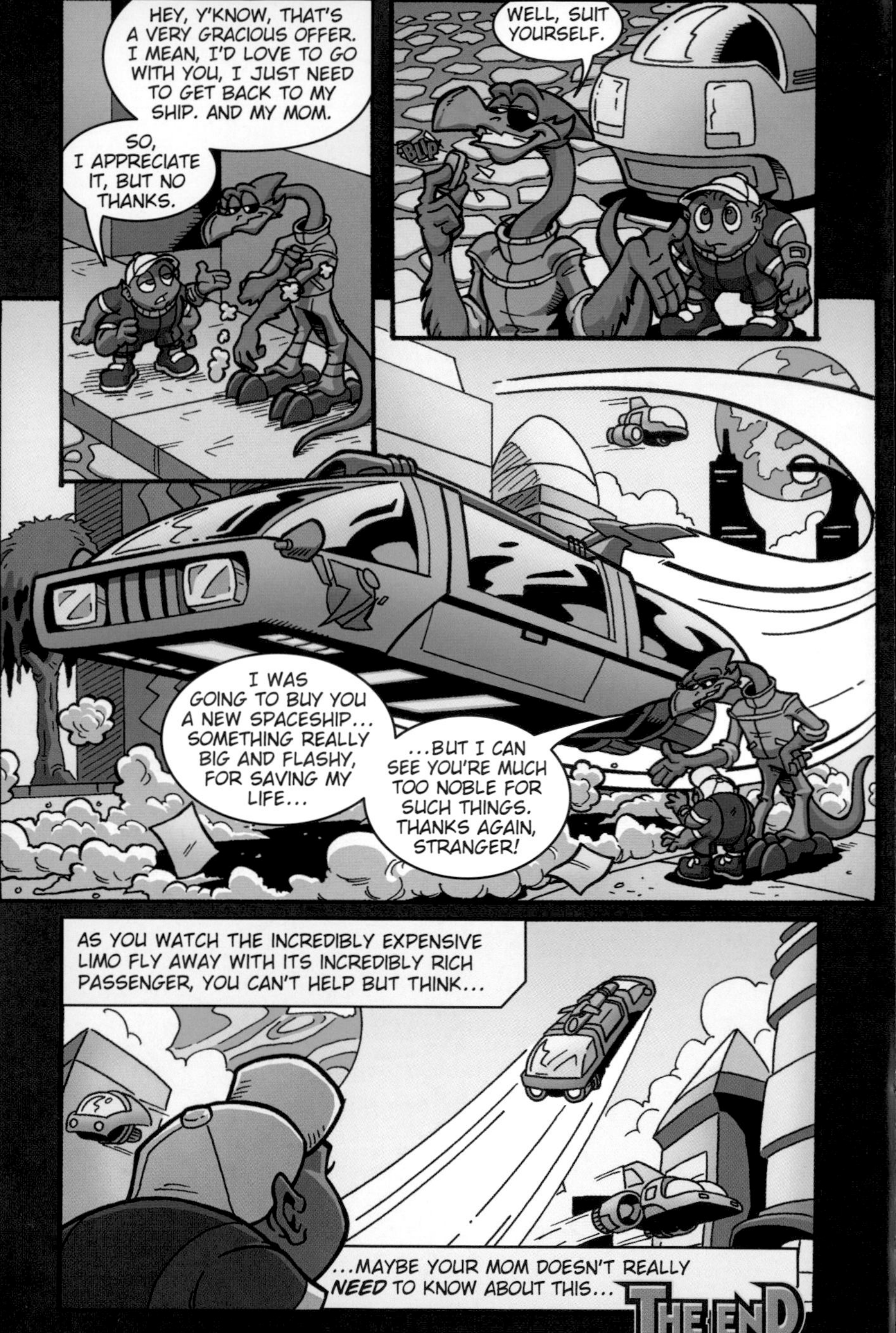
HEY, Y'KNOW, THAT'S A VERY GRACIOUS OFFER. I MEAN, I'D LOVE TO GO WITH YOU, I JUST NEED TO GET BACK TO MY SHIP. AND MY MOM.
SO, I APPRECIATE IT, BUT NO THANKS.
WELL, SUIT YOURSELF.
BLIP
I WAS GOING TO BUY YOU A NEW SPACESHIP... SOMETHING REALLY BIG AND FLASHY, FOR SAVING MY LIFE...
...BUT I CAN SEE YOU'RE MUCH TOO NOBLE FOR SUCH THINGS. THANKS AGAIN, STRANGER!
AS YOU WATCH THE INCREDIBLY EXPENSIVE LIMO FLY AWAY WITH ITS INCREDIBLY RICH PASSENGER, YOU CAN'T HELP BUT THINK...
...MAYBE YOUR MOM DOESN'T REALLY *NEED* TO KNOW ABOUT THIS...
THE END

"I don't want to take any chances," you tell Honest Broknuk. "Let's just sit back here and wait."

He agrees with you, of course, so the two of you stay quiet. You can hear the two Frongo thugs out in the store, banging around. The banging gets louder and louder, and then . . .

. . . the door to the back room bursts open. Kilippy stands there with his gun aimed straight at you and a snarl on his face. "Ten credits? *Ten credits?* That's all I get? You picked the wrong day to get cheap, old man! I think I need to make examples out of both of you!"

And as the Frongo sets his gun to "wide angle" and opens fire, you *really* wish you had tried to do something . . . !

THE END

Your mother didn't raise a fool! You spin on your heel, ready to sprint away from whatever weirdness is going on . . .

. . . but before you can even take the first step, a long, segmented arm reaches out of the darkness and grabs you around the waist. You struggle, but you can't break free, and the arm begins pulling you back . . . back toward those creepy eyes. You think you can hear jaws snapping together . . . !

GO ON TO THE NEXT PAGE.

You can't get away from this thing!

WILL YOU . . .

. . . stop struggling and yell, "Wait! I'm human!"?
TURN TO PAGE 102.

. . . fight even harder to break free of its grip?
TURN TO PAGE 111.

"Y'know, I can't believe I'm saying this, but . . . yeah, sure, I'll help you. What do you need me to do? You don't have to stick me with that gigantic needle, do you?"

"Oh, no, no-no-no," Dr. Sprigmarsh says. "The needle isn't necessary, because, well . . . the serum isn't even in it."

"All right . . . then where *is* the serum?"

He clears his throat nervously. "It was in that soda you just drank."

You would be getting really, really angry right about now—except that you start to feel weird. *Extremely* weird. You hold one hand up and, even through the disguise, you can tell that it's starting to *change*.

You start to panic . . . but wait! You might be able to *control* the change. It's sort of like playing with clay—except you're molding and shaping your hand just by *thinking* about it! You turn off your holo-projector so you can see what's happening to you.

GO ON TO THE NEXT PAGE.

Your body is transforming! But you
might be able to control the change.

WILL YOU . . .

. . . try really hard to stay human?
TURN TO PAGE 109.

. . . see what else you
can turn into?
TURN TO PAGE 83.

IF YOU TRY TO USE THE PHONE, THEY'LL PROBABLY HEAR YOU.

AND YOU *CERTAINLY* DON'T WANT TO SNEAK INTO THE ROOM BY YOURSELF!

SO THAT LEAVES THIS BIG RED BUTTON. WHAT IS IT? A PANIC BUTTON?

A DISTRESS SIGNAL? A GARAGE DOOR OPENER?

BLAARP

BLAARP

GAAAAH! FIRE! *FIRE!*

BLAARP

GO ON TO THE NEXT PAGE.

The storeroom door slams open with a huge crash, and the three criminals rush in—and go right past you.

"I don't want to die!" the Frongo yells. "What do we do? What do we do?"

"There!" The Zirifubi points toward the window you crawled in through. "Everybody out!"

All three of them dash toward the window and fling themselves through it. You hear three splashes from below. Curious, you go over to the window and look out . . .

. . . just in time to see a huge, hideous creature coming up from the bottom of the canal. The three criminals never know what hit them as the creature swallows them whole—*gulp gulp gulp.*

Holy zigunja! you think. *Glad I got out of the water when I did!*

TURN TO PAGE 19.

"Wait!" you shout. "Don't hurt me! I'm human!"

The arm spins you around. "Human?" a gruff voice demands. "What are you babbling about?"

"Here, I'll show you!" You gladly switch off the holo-projector and pull back your hood. "See? I'm a human! More specifically, I'm a human *child*."

The big Makaknuk lets you go, and then two others step out of the shadows, surrounding you. They all stare down at you with big, scary eyes.

"Human," the first one says. "Hmmm. I've never had human for supper before."

"Yeah," one of the others chimes in. "After a full day of robbing banks, I've really worked up an appetite."

They all pull out big, nasty-looking knives . . . and you realize that, for you, this is

THE END

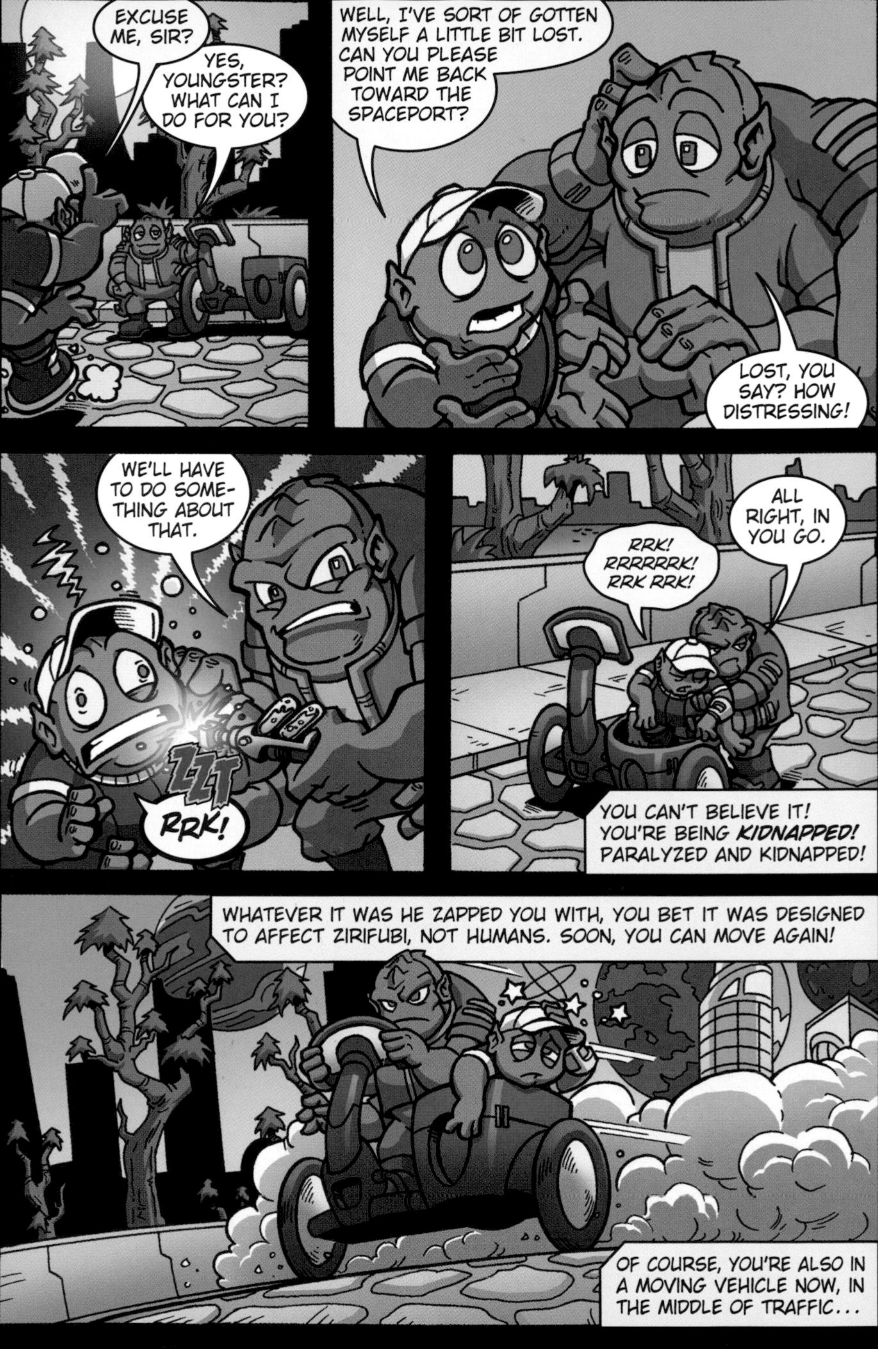

EXCUSE ME, SIR?
YES, YOUNGSTER? WHAT CAN I DO FOR YOU?
WELL, I'VE SORT OF GOTTEN MYSELF A LITTLE BIT LOST. CAN YOU PLEASE POINT ME BACK TOWARD THE SPACEPORT?
LOST, YOU SAY? HOW DISTRESSING!
WE'LL HAVE TO DO SOME-THING ABOUT THAT.
ZZT
RRK!
RRK! RRRRRRK! RRK RRK!
ALL RIGHT, IN YOU GO.
YOU CAN'T BELIEVE IT! YOU'RE BEING KIDNAPPED! PARALYZED AND KIDNAPPED!
WHATEVER IT WAS HE ZAPPED YOU WITH, YOU BET IT WAS DESIGNED TO AFFECT ZIRIFUBI, NOT HUMANS. SOON, YOU CAN MOVE AGAIN!
OF COURSE, YOU'RE ALSO IN A MOVING VEHICLE NOW, IN THE MIDDLE OF TRAFFIC...

GO ON TO THE NEXT PAGE.

You want to get away from this guy . . .
but you haven't had very good luck so far
falling off moving vehicles.

WILL YOU . . .

. . . wait till he stops to make your escape?
TURN TO PAGE 74.

. . . throw caution to the wind
and jump out now?
TURN TO PAGE 14.

"Look, Doc, I don't really like needles," you tell him, edging closer. You keep your eye on that big syringe in his hand.

"Well, I suppose I could find some alternative method of administering the—*hey!*"

Dr. Sprigmarsh shouts because you've just darted forward and grabbed the syringe right out of his grasp. "I bet the police will be very interested in this!" you yell as you sprint for the closest door you see.

"Steal from me, will you, you little *brat?!*" You glance back as you're running—and let out a yelp as you see Giorgio barreling toward you! "Get that child!" Dr. Sprigmarsh bellows.

You try to outrun the robot, but he's so *fast!* The last thing you see before Giorgio's metal hands close around your throat is the doorknob.

Just out of reach.

THE END

You creep out. The two Frongo thugs don't know you're there yet. They're still up at the front, trying to open the safe. There are gadgets all around you—maybe you can use one of them to bluff the Frongo.

You pick up a weird-looking hexagonal box. You don't know what it is . . . but then, you don't know what *any* of this stuff is. You move silently so that you're standing behind a shelf, then aim the box at them.

"Drop your guns!" you shout, and they look around at you—and before you realize what's happening, the box fires a beam of blue light. It surrounds the Frongo, and suddenly they're *frozen solid*.

Honest Broknuk calls the police. He gives you a really good discount on the wormhole analyzer . . . plus you'll also be getting a police commendation!

THE END

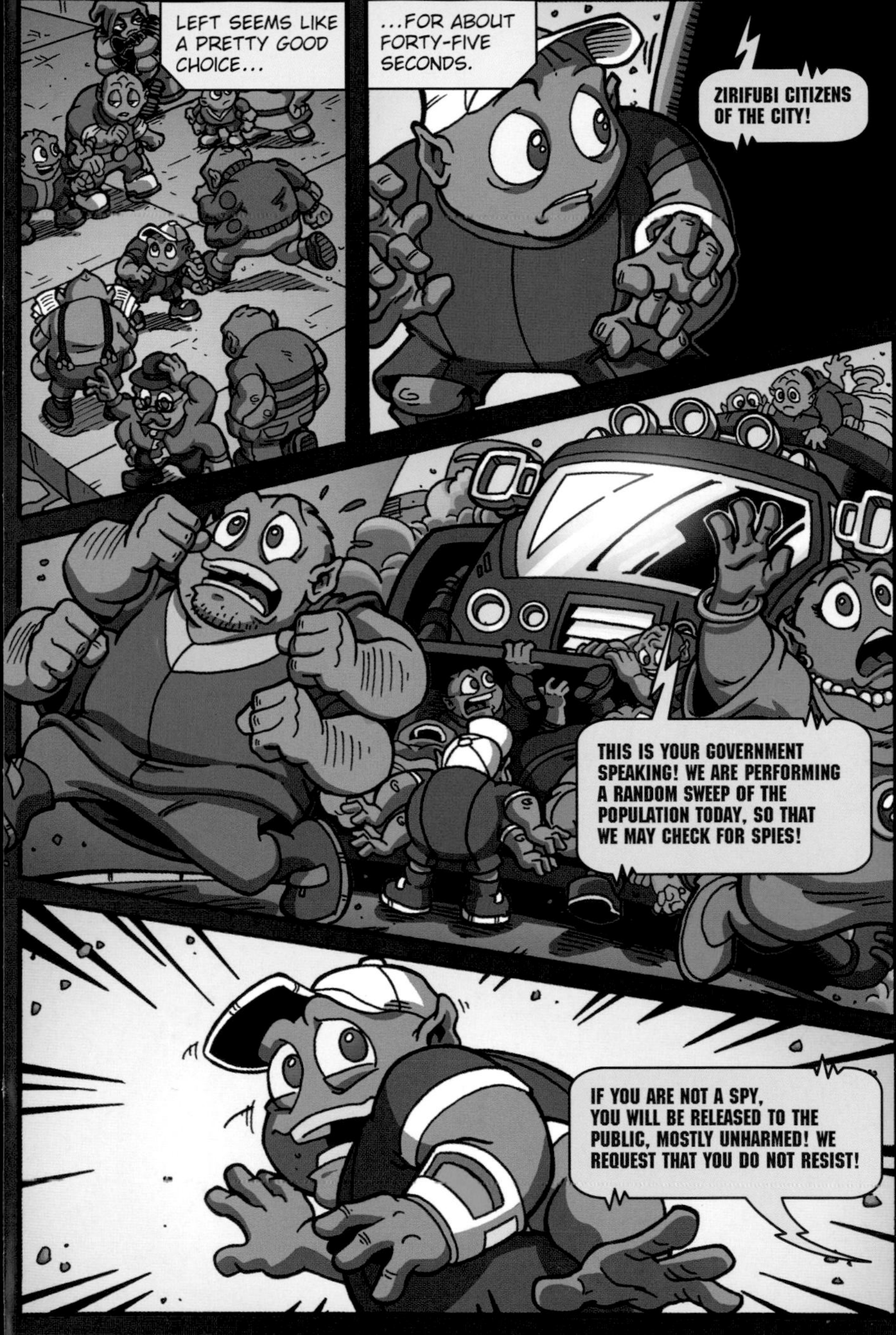
LEFT SEEMS LIKE A PRETTY GOOD CHOICE...
...FOR ABOUT FORTY-FIVE SECONDS.
ZIRIFUBI CITIZENS OF THE CITY!
THIS IS YOUR GOVERNMENT SPEAKING! WE ARE PERFORMING A RANDOM SWEEP OF THE POPULATION TODAY, SO THAT WE MAY CHECK FOR SPIES!
IF YOU ARE NOT A SPY, YOU WILL BE RELEASED TO THE PUBLIC, MOSTLY UNHARMED! WE REQUEST THAT YOU DO NOT RESIST!

GO ON TO THE NEXT PAGE.

You certainly don't want to get picked up
in a search for spies! Not while you're
wearing a disguise like this, anyway.

WILL YOU . . .

. . . take off running and try to
stay ahead of the machine?
TURN TO PAGE 25.

. . . count on being able to call
your mom, and surrender?
TURN TO PAGE 43.

You grit your teeth and concentrate as hard as you can. *I'm staying human! I'm* not *turning into anything gross!*

Slowly you feel the effects of whatever Dr. Sprigmarsh gave you fading away. Your hands start to feel normal again. You turn and face the doctor . . . who looks *very* embarrassed.

"I can't believe you did that!" you shout. "You *tricked* me into drinking your weird gene-mutation serum? That's just *wrong*!"

Dr. Sprigmarsh shoves a *huge* wad of cash into your hands and guides you toward the door, babbling, "Yes well you've provided me with some valuable data yes thank you very much must get back to my experiments now and of course there's *no* reason to sue no harm no foul so have a good day."

Suddenly you're through the door and outside. The door locks behind you.

Well, *that* was abrupt! But you're human. And you've got a *lot* of money. Wait till your mom sees the wormhole analyzer you can buy with this!

THE END

You're getting *really* tired of falling through all this weird alien stuff! But you land on a pile of something soft. It's too dark to see what it is, and you don't think you want to know. So you feel your way to a wall, and from there you find a door.

Outside the room, you see you're in a system of service tunnels. *There's got to be a way out,* you tell yourself, and you head down the nearest tunnel. You start to pass doors with signs beside them. "Discarded Clothing." "Discarded Toothbrushes." "Discarded Bicycle Chains." *Wow, they're really specific!*

Then you see a sign that makes you laugh out loud. "Discarded Spaceship Parts." Inside the room, you find a pile of used wormhole analyzers! Unwanted, yours for the taking. Some of them look pretty new too!

Now, you just have to figure out how to get out of here and call your mother . . .

THE END

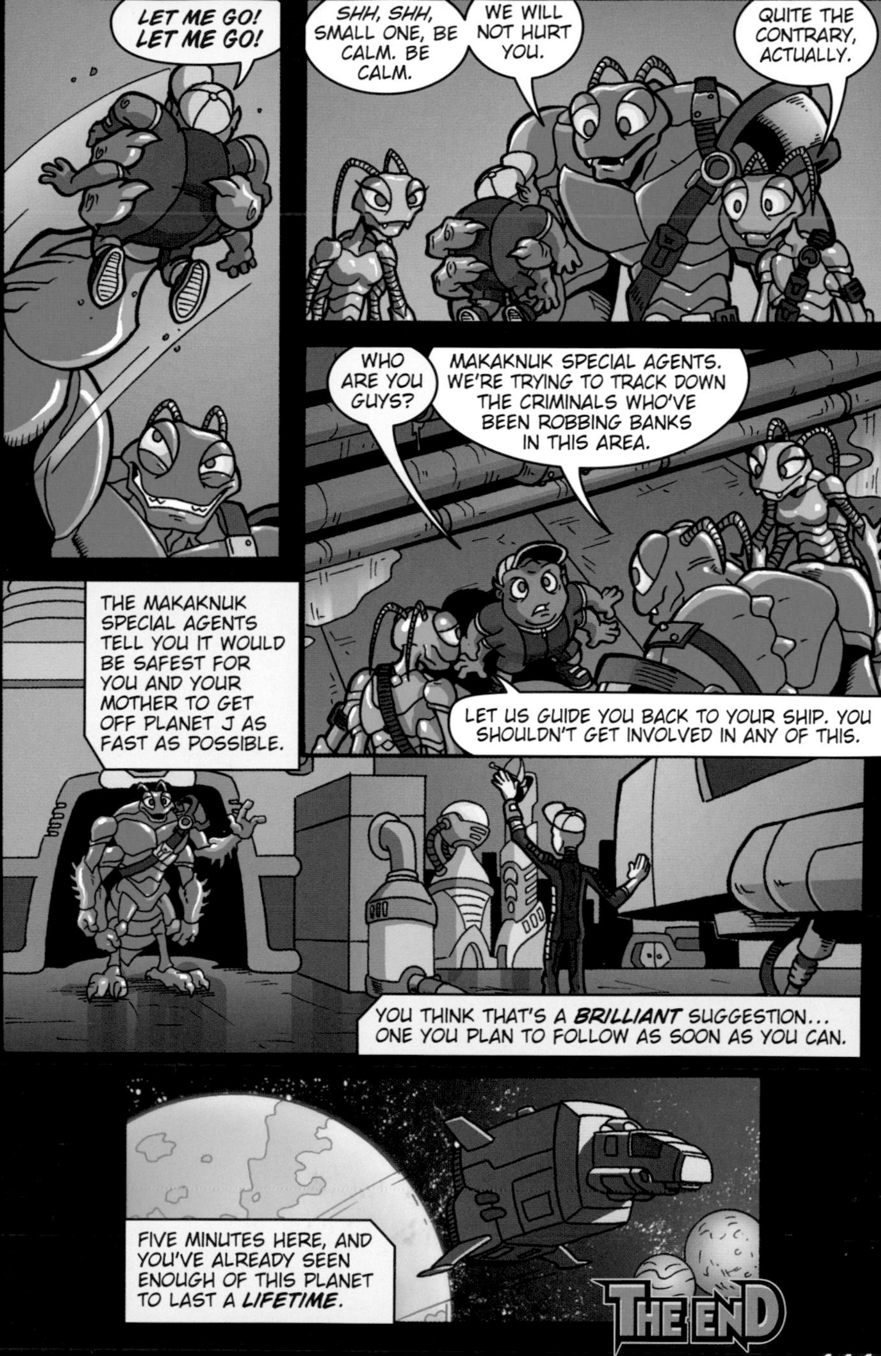
LET ME GO! LET ME GO!
SHH, SHH, SMALL ONE, BE CALM. BE CALM.
WE WILL NOT HURT YOU.
QUITE THE CONTRARY, ACTUALLY.
WHO ARE YOU GUYS?
MAKAKNUK SPECIAL AGENTS. WE'RE TRYING TO TRACK DOWN THE CRIMINALS WHO'VE BEEN ROBBING BANKS IN THIS AREA.
THE MAKAKNUK SPECIAL AGENTS TELL YOU IT WOULD BE SAFEST FOR YOU AND YOUR MOTHER TO GET OFF PLANET J AS FAST AS POSSIBLE.
LET US GUIDE YOU BACK TO YOUR SHIP. YOU SHOULDN'T GET INVOLVED IN ANY OF THIS.
YOU THINK THAT'S A *BRILLIANT* SUGGESTION... ONE YOU PLAN TO FOLLOW AS SOON AS YOU CAN.
FIVE MINUTES HERE, AND YOU'VE ALREADY SEEN ENOUGH OF THIS PLANET TO LAST A *LIFETIME*.
THE END

WHICH TWISTED JOURNEYS® WILL YOU TRY NEXT?

#1 CAPTURED BY PIRATES
A band of scurvy pirates has boarded your ship. Can you keep them from turning you into shark bait?

#2 ESCAPE FROM PYRAMID X
You're on a visit to a pyramid, complete with ancient mummies. But not everything that's ancient is dead . . .

#3 TERROR IN GHOST MANSION
You're trapped in a creepy old house on Halloween with a bunch of spooks. And they aren't wearing costumes . . .

#4 THE TREASURE OF MOUNT FATE
Can you survive the monsters and magic of Mount Fate and bring home its treasure?

#5 NIGHTMARE ON ZOMBIE ISLAND
Legend says no one escapes Zombie Island. Will you be the first? Or will this nightmare be your last?

#6 THE TIME TRAVEL TRAP
Dinosaurs, Wild West train robbers, robots . . . Danger is everywhere when you're caught in a time machine!

#7 VAMPIRE HUNT
Vampire hunters are creeping through an ancient castle. And you're the vampire they're hunting!

#8 ALIEN INCIDENT ON PLANET J
Make peace with the Makaknuk, Zirifubi, and Frongo, or you'll never get off their planet . . .